CASTOFF COWHAND

Trevor Killian was the sort of cowboy it was easy to overlook or forget, so whenever work slowed down, the ranchers always let him go first. However, Alton Huxford wasn't likely to forget him, for Trevor saved him from being lynched. From that moment on he became the only ray of hope for the Huxford family and their small, troubled ranch. But could he and the Huxfords have any chance against the massive Scythe ranch? As the battle lines are drawn, Trevor finds an unexpected ally . . .

BILLY HALL

CASTOFF COWHAND

Complete and Unabridged

LINFORD
Leicester

First published in Great Britain in 2002 by
Robert Hale Limited
London

First Linford Edition
published 2003
by arrangement with
Robert Hale Limited
London

British Library CIP Data

Hall, Billy
    Castoff cowhand.—Large print ed.—
    Linford western library
    1. Western stories
    2. Large type books
    I. Title
    823.9′14 [F]

    ISBN 1–8439–5028–6

1

Trevor Killian stood in his stirrups. He eased the gun in its holster, and inched forward through the thick stand of trees. At the edge of the timber he strained to see and hear. He was far too experienced to step into something until he knew exactly what was going on.

'Looks like a Scythe cow to me,' a coarse voice growled. Trevor sized up the cowboy, sitting with his back to his vantage point.

The answer came from a softer voice, out of sight behind the two horsemen. It was slightly tainted with fear. 'All you have to do is check her brand.'

The second mounted cowboy answered. 'I can't see no brand. Can you, Hank?'

The softer voice responded. His

words were beginning to carry a tone of desperation. 'Well, of course not. I have her tied down, and the brand's on the bottom. Let me roll her over and I'll show you.'

Hank spoke again. 'Aw, no need to do that. That's one of our cows, sure's anything. It's one of ours, and here you are, just a-waitin' fer her calf to drop so you can stick your brand on it.'

'The calf is breached. I tied her up to try to get it turned around. See, those are its hind legs sticking out.'

'Yeah, they's hind legs, all right, but that there's a Scythe cow, sure's anything.'

'Whatd'ya think, Windy? Reckon we oughta just string 'im up?'

Windy spat a brown streak of tobacco juice. 'Seems the only thing to do,' he responded.

Trevor silently slid his thirty-thirty out of its saddle scabbard. He used the gun barrel to part the branches that still separated him from the scene in the clearing. When the gun was levelled, he worked the lever to jack a shell into the chamber.

The effect of the sound was electric. Both mounted cowboys stiffened as if they had suddenly been backed against a post. The man on the ground stepped sideways to peer past the two mounted cowboys.

Trevor spoke. 'Seems to me it might make sense to check that brand, afore you boys go hangin' a man fer rustlin'.'

He could see the two cowboys trying to look at each other without moving their heads. It was Windy who finally spoke. 'Who are you? Why are you buyin' into this affair?'

Trevor answered with a question of his own. 'Who are you boys, and why are you so anxious to hang this fella?'

Windy gathered himself and started to turn. Trevor's sharp voice froze him where he stood. 'Don't even think about turnin' around. An' drop them guns on the ground, afore I see you twitch an' think you're fixin' to try somethin'. Drop 'em! Now!'

Both men dropped their guns, jerking their hands back as if the guns had suddenly become too hot to hold.

'Now let's try again,' Trevor said. His voice was slow and even, but edged with steel. 'Who are you boys, and why are you so anxious to hang this fella?'

Windy was all too glad to be the spokesman. 'Why, we're hands of the Scythe Ranch. We're just out here doin' our job, fulfilling the just and proper obligations of the sooth and substance of our employment, checking the cows for the spread which provides sustenance — '

The man on the ground interrupted. 'This is H-X land, and this is an H-X cow. You ain't even on Scythe land.'

Windy was unperturbed. 'Well, now, we may not exactly be within the usual borders of what would be the Scythe Ranch, if you wanted to speak real technical-like, but this whole valley is more or less Scythe land, and we have a forsooth problem with some of these smaller ranchers branding our stock. It

4

happens all the time. It happens, in fact, with adjunct and faceted regularity in the vicinity of the H-X, which is why it behooves us to be riding hereabouts. Why, we have, within the past fortnight or maybe even less, beheld this phenomenon realize itself with adjunct and faceted repetition — '

Trevor cut in. 'So what makes you think this here's a Scythe cow?'

Windy had another breath. 'Well, it behooves us to behold the probability at once, when we see a personage who is a known perpetrator of such adjunct and faceted acts with an animal tied in a position that conceals her brand, attempting to brand a calf . . . '

'I don't see no brandin' iron. Nor no fire, neither.'

Windy paused for only a breath. 'Well, the fire may not have been kindled thereto perchance, but it only demonstrates the sooth of the intent that must surely have been there . . . '

'Roll 'er over,' Trevor commanded.

'What?'

'Roll 'er over. Dab a loop on her legs an' roll 'er over. Let's look.'

Hank and Windy looked quickly at each other. It was Hank who responded. 'Let's just ride.'

Trevor's voice barked, 'I said, roll 'er over. Windy, you do it. Hank, keep your hands where I can see 'em.'

The two cowboys looked at each other again. Then they shrugged, and Windy shook out a couple of coils of his lariat. He tossed a loop over the cow's three feet that were tied together with a short rope. He dallied the rope on his saddle horn and pulled the reins, nudging his horse with his heels. The horse backed, tightening the rope. The rope pulled the cow's legs up and over, turning her over on to her other side.

'Well, now,' Trevor said, 'that sure 'nough looks like an H-X brand to me. Now I wonder, does that mean this cow is an H-X cow, or does that mean that it's really a Scythe cow just pretendin' to belong to the H-X? Or maybe it's one o' them there sooth cows you keep talkin' about. What's a sooth brand look like?'

Windy nudged his horse forward, slackening the rope. He tugged the loop off the cow's legs and recoiled the lariat, fastening it back on his saddle. 'Well, it does appear that we may have made a minor mistake, here — '

'It does appear you was lookin' fer a chance to hang a man fer nothin',' Trevor interrupted.

Trevor turned to the man standing on the ground. 'Who're you?'

'Alton Huxford. I own the H-X. This is my cow, and my calf, if I can get it pulled before it dies.'

'Why are these two boys so all-fired anxious to string you up?'

Huxford sighed heavily. His shoulders sagged, and his eyes were dull. A small spark flared as he looked at the two cowboys, but died again before he turned his eyes back to Trevor. 'Because they are Scythe Ranch hands, and they think they own the whole valley. They want my land, but I will not be

7

frightened off. That's why they decided to use this as an excuse to hang me, I guess. Then they could tell my wife how sorry they were after they found out it was my own cow.'

'You wanta hang 'em?'

The question caught all three men by surprise. The two cowboys whirled to stare in disbelief, and found themselves staring down the barrel of Trevor's thirty-thirty. They both swallowed, as if by the same impulse. Huxford stared at Trevor for a full minute before he answered. 'Why, no, I 'spect not. Make 'em leave their guns and send 'em home. I am not a killer.'

Trevor spoke to the pair. 'You heard 'im, boys. Shuck out them saddle guns an' ride out. And don't come back on H-X land unless you plan to bring a whole lot more boys than what you come with today.'

Both men drew the carbines from their scabbards and dropped them on the ground. Hank finally spoke. 'Who are you? Why are you buyin' into this?

It ain't none o' your doin's.'

'Well, ain't it now?' Trevor responded. 'I guess that's just fer me to know and you to wonder. Now ride!'

As he spoke, Trevor fired the rifle, shooting the tip off the right ear of Hank's horse. The animal shied violently, nearly unseating the cowboy. Then he shook his head and bucked twice. Hank swore and fought to regain control of the animal, sending it finally into a run. The animal kept shaking its head, and so failed to see a rock jutting out of the ground. It tripped on the rock and fell, spilling Hank headlong on to the ground, nearly falling on top of him.

Horse and rider scrambled to their feet. Swearing profusely, Hank leapt back into the saddle and jammed his spurs into the horse's sides. The horse surged forward into an all-out run, fleeing from the stinging of his ear as much as the pain of the spurs. Windy still sat where he had been, watching in open-mouthed stupor.

Trevor called him out of the trance. 'You just catchin' flies with your mouth open there, or you aimin' to ride out afore I wake your horse up too?'

Windy's jaw snapped shut. He looked at Trevor, then at the diminishing dust cloud left by Hank's fleeing mount. In uncharacteristic silence he spurred his horse and fled.

'Now why did you do that?' Huxford asked.

Trevor chuckled. 'Well, I ain't too sure. Seemed like a good idea at the time. Sure took away any idea either one had o' pullin' somethin', didn't it?'

Huxford joined in the chuckle. 'It did that, for a fact. He'll probably have another good ride the first time he tries to shoot off of that horse, too.'

'Oh, he'll be gun-shy, that's for sure,' Trevor agreed.

Huxford looked back at Trevor. 'I don't know who you are, but I'm much obliged. They'd have killed me, you know.'

'I sorta gathered that. You don't seem

10

too upset about it, though. I'd be mad enough to bite nails in two right now, if'n I was you.'

Huxford shrugged. 'I guess I got over bein' mad about it. I figure if the good Lord wants to let 'em kill me, there ain't much I can do about it. They seem pretty determined to get my land.'

'Crowdin' you off, huh?'

'They're trying. It might be better if I just give in and let them have it. I don't know what my family would do if they succeeded in killing me.'

'Where's your hands?'

'Don't have any. I just have a small spread here. Oh, I need a couple hands, at least. It's just that I've lost so many cattle I don't have anything to pay hands with, so we're just tryin' to run the place ourselves.'

'We? Who's we?'

'Oh me an' the missus, and we got two kids. Leah's fifteen. Stuart's eleven.'

Trevor's eyes took on a distant look. 'Old enough to be a lot o' help.

Leastwise I was at that age.'

'Oh Leah does well, for a girl,' Huxford said.

'I meant the boy. Eleven's old enough to be a hand.'

Huxford started to answer, then changed his mind. He looked back at the cow. 'I hate to impose on good nature, after you just saved my life, but I wonder if you'd mind giving me a hand. I need to roll that cow back over, then see if I can get that calf back in and turned around so she can have him. I'm gonna lose it an' the cow both if don't.'

'Looks that way,' Trevor agreed.

He rode from the trees into the clearing. He lowered the hammer on his rifle and stepped to the ground. Trevor laid the rifle on the ground within easy reach. Together they grasped the bound feet of the cow and rolled her back over. Her eyes rolled wildly at them. She bellowed, tongue hanging out the corner of her gaping mouth.

Without being asked further, Trevor

knelt behind the cow. Waiting until her contractions relaxed, he grasped the protruding feet of the calf and pushed, forcing the calf back into the cow. He continued to push until his arm was into the cow just past his elbow. He felt the calf slip back into the womb. Reaching in as far as he could, he grasped the calf and turned it until he found the head. Then he gripped the birth sac, moving it to the entrance to the womb, head first. Just as he did, the cow had another contraction, and the front feet and head moved into the birth canal. He removed his hand and arm and leaned back. It took only two more contractions for the cow to birth the calf. As the head appeared, Huxford moved quickly to untie the ropes binding three of the cow's legs together. Both men stepped clear. Trevor picked up his rifle and dropped it into his saddle scabbard. Each man moved to his horse. As though moved by the same impulse, each lifted a foot into the stirrup and stood there with the other foot on the ground, waiting to see whether the cow would charge them or tend to her new calf.

As soon as the calf emerged from the cow, she lumbered to her feet. She stood spraddle-legged, head hanging, for nearly two minutes. Then she gathered her feet under her and struggled for a couple of steps. She glared at the two men and tossed her head several times. Long strings of slobber flew from her mouth to land in the plentiful buffalo grass. Then she turned her attention to her new calf.

She shambled to the calf and began to lick it clean. Both men let out great sighs. 'She's a good ol' momma,' Huxford said. 'She'll forget all about us, now. They's a crick just over that little rise, if you wanta wash your arm off some.'

The two men walked together, leading their horses, to the edge of the creek. Trevor drew his thirty-thirty from its scabbard again. Before he knelt at the side of the creek, he took a long, careful look around. Only when he was satisfied the other two had not returned did he lay the weapon on the ground. Even then it stayed within easy reach.

Both men washed in the cold, clear water. When they were finished, they dried their hands and arms on their shirt tails, then tucked the shirts in again.

Trevor looked the rancher over. 'Runnin' the place without hands, huh?'

'Tryin'.'

'Tough way to run a spread. Now me, I'm sorta lookin' fer a job. How's the chance o' hirin' on?'

Huxford smiled ruefully. 'Well, I'd hire you in a minute, if I could. I already know you won't run from a fight. You're a good hand with stock. You turned that there breached calf easier'n anyone I ever saw. Like I say, I'd hire you in a minute if I could. I just ain't got nothin' to pay you with.'

'How's your calf crop look?'

'Oh, it looks great! We had a real soft,

open winter. Stock weathered real good. I ain't found an open cow in the herd. If I can get 'em took care of, I'll have the best calf crop I ever had in my life.'

Trevor studied the rancher's face.

'Well, how about if I hired on, an' you didn't have to pay me nothin' till you sell the calves?'

Hope brought a spark to the dull resignation of the rancher's eyes. 'You'd do that? You'd hire on without wages till I sell this year's calves?'

Trevor shrugged. 'Well, I might need a little tobaccy money, time to time. Somethin' like that. But I can do without very much money at all, long's you're keepin' me fed.'

'You're hired!' Huxford enthused.

'Well, then, let's get busy an' check the rest o' the herd,' Trevor said, stepping into the saddle. Then he added, 'boss.'

2

Both men slouched in the saddle. The sun was just dropping behind the Big Horn Mountains to their west. Even the horses walked with a shambling gait, speeding only slightly as they began that last mile towards home.

'That was some day!' Alton exulted.

Trevor smiled. 'It was that. What did we count? Twenty-eight new calves?'

'Twenty-seven,' Alton corrected. 'And all up an' suckin'. Every one. Even the one you pushed back 'n turned. Twenty-seven new calves, two o' Pashenka's boys run off, an' me with a new hand! Wow! What a day!'

'I feel like I put in a day, too,' Trevor lamented. 'I ain't done a good day's work for a couple months. It'll take me a week or so to get back in shape, I reckon.'

'Where'd you winter?'

Trevor's mouth tightened and his eyes narrowed, but otherwise his expression did not change. 'Up by Meeteetse.'

'Cow outfit?'

'Yup. I worked for the Lantern-R.'

'I've heard of it. Clemson that runs it, ain't it?'

'Yup.'

'Odd sort, I've heard. Why'd you quit?'

Trevor's jaw tightened. His lips narrowed. 'I didn't. Got my walkin' papers.'

Huxford's voice betrayed a conflict between courtesy and feeling this might be something about his newly-hired hand he ought to know. 'How'd you come to do that just ahead of calvin'? That's usually the easiest time to hire on, not get let go.'

The muscles at the hinge of Trevor's jaw bunched again. 'Yeah, usually. Three old hands showed up from somewheres. Seems they had some sort o' tie with the boss from when they worked there before. He didn't need that many hands, so he let me go so he could hire all three of 'em.'

'Is that a fact? That ain't a very fair shake, is it?'

Trevor's jaw relaxed and he smiled tightly. 'Nope. I didn't think so. I'm sorta used to it, though. I seem to be one o' them sort o' people that's easy to get rid of. There's people that are like that, you know? Like one o' them people you notice sometimes, in a crowd o' people, an' afterward you try to remember, and you can remember everyone in the crowd but that one. You know there was one more person there, but you can't never remember him. No matter where that fella goes, it seems like he's just real easy to forget. I guess I must be like that. Folks sorta find it easy to put me outa mind.'

'Did Clemson pay you what you had comin'?'

'Oh yeah. Fact is, he paid me most of a month extra. Like maybe he felt like he was givin' me the short end o' the stick, so he paid me a little extra to make up fer it. That's why I said I could work fer ya till you sell your calves without gettin' paid. I got quite a bit. 'Sides, if I'm workin', I ain't hangin' around town spendin' money, so it won't take as much. By the time you sell them calves, I oughta have a halfway decent stake comin'.'

Huxford nodded. They topped a hill and came into sight of the H-X ranch buildings. As if on some silent signal, they both pulled their horses to a stop. They sat there studying the lay of the ranch in front of and slightly below them.

The ranch house sat at the very top of a low hill, in a large area clear of timber. It was built partly of logs, partly of rock, and some small amounts of cut lumber. The unlikely combination of materials was blended together in such a way that the whole house looked carefully planned, perfectly integrated and attractive. A low porch ran across the entire western front of the house, with a panoramic view of the Big Horn Mountains spread out before it. Every room of the house had at least one window of real glass, and most appeared to have two or three. The glass reflected the warm, red glow of the lowering sun, giving the house the appearance of a gem, reflecting light in glowing rays.

The barn was north of the house, at nearly fifty yards distant. It was on lower ground, so the house appeared to tower over it. About fifty feet from the house, a low hedge of plum bushes formed a line to separate the house's yard from the rest of the ranch yard. It was low enough so the barn could be seen from the house, but it made a clear and obvious break between the two.

The corrals were large and well built. The bunkhouse sat east of both house and barn. It was between the two, on lower ground than the house, but higher than the barn. The house and the bunkhouse had separate outhouses. The one for the bunkhouse was between it and the barn, in view of any of the three buildings. The outhouse for the occupants of the house was on the opposite side from the bunkhouse, so anyone going to or coming from it could not be seen from either the bunkhouse or barn.

There was another addition to the house built on a lower level than the rest of the building. It reached out towards the bunkhouse, forming a room that appeared to be about fifteen by thirty feet. Trevor instantly surmised it was either a cookhouse or a chow hall for the hands to eat. He guessed there must be two or three interior steps to move from the house down into it.

His lips tightened again as he studied the layout of the buildings. The indicators were subtle, but very definite. Nobody who worked on the H-X ranch would be likely to forget that they were on a lower level than the owners. The reminders were consistent, and the layout of the yard ingenious to that end.

'Who laid out the buildings?' Trevor asked, working to keep his voice even and neutral.

'Oh, Vinny did that. That's my wife. Her name's Lavina, but I just call her Vinny. I never did figure out what was so all-fired important about just where each building had to be put, but she likes it this way. I always figured if you could get from one building to the other, it didn't make much difference where they sat. Well, as long as the house ain't usually downwind from the barn, that is. Anyway, Vinny likes it this way. The house is a little harder to heat in the winter, what with sittin' up there on top where the wind gets a clean sweep at it, but I built 'er pretty tight. She ain't too hard to keep warm. Takes a little extra wood when the wind blows, is all.'

Again, as if on some silent signal, both men lifted their reins and nudged their horses into motion. The animals responded with quickening gait as they headed towards the familiar barn. They unsaddled and took care of their animals inside.

'We'll just put 'em in stalls for tonight, and grain 'em a little, along with some hay,' Huxford said. 'Tomorrow we'll run the *remuda* in the corral and you can pick yourself a string o' horses. You'll probably need half a dozen. I got upwards o' forty-five head, so you won't have any trouble pickin' good ones. You might get some that ain't been ridden for a while, is all.'

'That's all right,' Trevor said at once. 'I don't mind; that way I can get 'em broke into workin' the way I like 'em to. I don't mind even startin' from scratch with two or three, if there's any raw broncs in the bunch.'

'There's several,' Huxford acknowledged. 'Since I let the hands go last year, I've been tryin' to do things myself, mostly. That don't leave much time for breakin' any extra horses.'

'I 'spect not, all right.'

'Well, come on. Let's go up to the house and I'll introduce you to my

24

family, and we'll see if Vinny ain't got supper about ready.'

By the time they had walked up the hill to the house, Trevor was fighting a sense of irritation. Riding boots weren't made for walking, and having to walk such a distance up that much of a hill every time a trip had to be made from the barn to the house didn't make sense to him. It especially made no sense if it were, as it appeared to be, all done for the sake of vanity. Most ranchers and their families in this county considered themselves equals with their hands. They didn't always socialize together, but at barn dances, community affairs, box socials and all such things, they did. They certainly didn't go out of their way to flaunt some supposed superiority. With an effort, he forced the thoughts from his mind.

As they approached the front door Trevor was once again impressed with the house. The door was built of heavy planks, hung on large strap hinges, and was more than two inches thick. It must have weighed well over a hundred pounds, but when Huxford opened it, it moved easily and silently. He called out to his family. 'Vinny, Leah, Stuart, come meet our new hand.'

As the family assembled, he introduced them. 'This here is Trevor Killian. He saved my bacon today. He stood up to two of Pashenka's hands, and run 'em off when they had me backed down pretty good.'

Trevor saw the alarm leap to Lavina's eyes as she darted looks back and forth between her husband and him. The children's eyes only grew large and eager, as if about to hear some marvellous story. It was Lavina who spoke. 'What happened? Who was it?'

'Aw, it was that Windy fella that always uses them big words, and the big guy that growls like a bear when he talks. Hank, I guess his name is. I was fixin' to pull a calf, and they accused me of waiting for a Scythe cow to calve so I could steal the calf. But it was one of ours.'

'What happened?' Lavina repeated.

'Well, we was jawin', and they started threatenin' to hang me . . . '

He had to pause for a moment at Lavina's gasp. Her hands flew to her mouth, but she said nothing more, so he continued. 'Then Trevor yelled at 'em from the trees, an' made 'em toss their guns down and ride off. Then he pushed back a breached calf and turned it around so the ol' cow had it slicker'n a whistle. So I know he's a good hand with cows, and he can stand up to the Scythe, and he agreed to hire on with us, so we got a new hand.'

Lavina's eyes darted back and forth between the two men for another moment, then she seemed to collect herself and remember her manners. She lowered her hands from her mouth and wiped them on her apron. She took a deep breath, let it out slowly, then looked back at Trevor. 'Well, I'm sure we'll have some more questions about that, but they will wait. I am pleased to meet you, Mr Killian.'

As she spoke, she extended a hand to him. Instead of holding the hand out in a position to be shaken, she held it out palm downward, hanging somewhat limply, as though she expected him to kiss it or something. Trevor hesitated, then took the hand, held it briefly and released it. 'Glad to meetcha, Ma'am,' he mumbled.

'Well,' Lavina said again. 'It is normally our custom for the hands to eat in their own dining room, but since you are the only hand we have at the moment, that would seem to be impractical. You will sleep in the bunkhouse, of course, but you may take your meals with us.'

She turned to the girl. As she did, her voice took on a different, harsher tone. 'Leah! Don't stand there with your mouth open. Get busy and put another place at the table for Mr Killian. You should have done that already. Can't you think of anything by yourself? Now hurry up. Get it done.'

Leah shot a look towards Trevor from

under her lowered lashes, and turned to do as her mother had bidden.

Stuart spoke to Trevor. 'Are you a gunfighter?'

Trevor laughed. 'No, I ain't no gunfighter. I'm just a down-at-the-heels cowpoke.'

'You got a gun?'

Lavina turned to the boy. 'Stuart, it is not polite to ask such questions of a grown-up. Now get in there and get your hands washed for supper.'

'I already warshed,' Stuart protested.

'Washed! Washed!' Lavina corrected. 'There is no 'r' in wash. Just because we live in the wilderness is no reason to speak like a barbarian.'

'I just talk like everybody else.'

'If everybody in the area spoke backwards, would you speak backwards too just because everybody else did?'

Stuart thought about it. 'Well, yeah, I s'pose. If everybody talked that way then that's the way everybody'd understand too, so I guess that'd be the right way, then.'

Trevor fought to hide the grin that threatened to control his face. Lavina's voice rose half an octave and several decibels. 'Don't you sass me, young man, or I'll have your father take a belt to you! You do not talk to me that way! Now get over to the table and sit down and I don't want to hear one more word from you until supper is finished. If I do, you'll go to bed without supper. Do you understand me?'

'Yes, Ma'am,' Stuart mumbled in a resigned tone. He shuffled to the table and sat down.

Alton nodded to Trevor. 'Come on, Trevor. I'll show you where to wash up, and we'll eat.'

When they were seated they all looked expectantly to Alton. He cleared his throat and looked at Trevor. 'Uh, we always start our meal with sayin' grace.'

Trevor nodded and bowed his head. Alton said a brief word of thanks. As he said 'Amen,' Leah reached out and grabbed the platter of meat. A loud 'smack' ensued as Lavina slapped her hand. She jerked the hand back and looked at her mother with offended eyes, brimming with tears. Lavina's voice was intense. 'What's the matter with you? Don't you have any manners at all? When we have company, the food is passed to them first. How many times have I told you that?'

'But that's what I was going to do! I was picking it up to pass it to him,' Leah protested.

'Oh, don't tell me that!' Lavina rejected. 'Don't sit there and tell me you were being anything but your usual selfish, thoughtless self. You never in your life did anything polite without me forcing you to. Now pass the meat to Mr Killian.'

'Please just call me Trevor,' Trevor requested. 'And go ahead and help yourselves. If I'm workin' fer the outfit, I can't rightly be considered company, so you all oughta go ahead and help yourselves first nohow.'

'Anyhow,' Stuart corrected.

Another loud smack ensued as

Lavina slapped Stuart on the shoulder. 'You do not correct company,' she admonished. 'Especially with a correction that is just as wrong as what he said. The word is anyway.'

'Anyway, pass the spuds,' Alton interrupted.

Lavina glared at him, but did not respond. A large bowl of soup was passed around, and each transferred some to a bowl beside their plate. In addition, there was roast beef, boiled potatoes, and some kind of greens Trevor thought must be lamb's quarters. The room fell silent as they all became intent on eating.

Lavina suddenly reached out and clubbed Leah on the shoulder with her forearm, causing her to slop some of the soup she was eating.

'Stop slurping! You sound like a hog or something.'

Leah's face reddened, but she said nothing. Alton looked uncomfortable as well, but he, too, kept his silence.

Lavina kept at it. 'I don't know how

old you're going to be before you learn decent manners. I'm ashamed to have anyone over for a meal, with you at the table.'

Trevor could hold his peace no longer. 'That was probably me that slurped the soup. I'm sorry.'

Lavina would have none of it. 'No it wasn't. It was Leah. She's such a slob. I've tried and tried to teach her decent manners, but she's just a slob. Look at her fingernails. Did you ever see such dirty fingernails on a girl?'

'Momma,' Leah protested, 'I was plantin' strawberries like you tol' me to. You wouldn't give me time to clean 'em before supper. Digging in the dirt always makes my hands look like that.'

Lavina's voice raised several decibels. 'Don't talk back to me in that tone of voice, you little brat! I'll slap you right across the mouth!'

Alton finally spoke up. His voice was almost plaintive, but firm. 'Leave 'er be, Vinny. She didn't mean nothin' by it.'

Lavina looked like she was about to

explode. She glared at her husband, then glanced at Trevor. She opened her mouth twice to speak, but shut it again both times. She put her hands in her lap and said nothing. She made no effort to continue her own supper.

The rest ate in strained silence. Lavina sat and stared at nothing throughout the rest of the meal. As soon as they were finished, Lavina rose and silently began clearing the table. Stuart beat a hasty retreat from the room, and Leah rose to follow him. She was hauled up short by her mother's voice. 'Leah! Get right back in here. You're not going anywhere until the table is cleared and these dishes are done. In fact, just for being so sneaky and lazy and trying to skulk out without helping, you can do it all yourself. I'm going to sit out on the porch for a little while, and rest. I've been working like a mule the whole day trying to get things done for this family, and you haven't hardly lifted a finger to help. Now you can just finish up by yourself.'

'But, Momma! I been working all day, too!'

'Shut up and get busy or I'll really give you a day's worth of work to do tomorrow. You're so lazy you couldn't do one whole day's work if your life depended on it. Now stop your bellyaching and whining and get busy. I'll be back in a little bit, and this kitchen had better be spotless!'

Trevor looked at Alton. The rancher appeared embarrassed, but he said nothing. Trevor reached for his hat. 'Thank you for the supper, Mrs Huxford,' he said. 'It was a real fine meal. I 'spect I'll go down to the barn and get my stuff and find a bunk in the bunkhouse.'

'Breakfast is at five,' Lavina said. She turned her back to him and walked out on to the porch.

Without another word from anyone, Trevor made his exit. He was stopped by Stuart. 'Can I come with you, Trevor?'

Trevor glanced up towards Lavina

but she was ignoring everyone. He looked at Alton, who merely shrugged. 'Why sure,' he told Stuart. 'I'd like that a lot. I could use someone to show me around the place a little.'

He and the boy walked down the hill towards the barn. The boy's chatter, interspersed with Trevor's quiet drawl, drifted back up through the quiet evening air.

3

'I ain't never seen nobody fence off a separate place just fer horses.'

Alton Huxford smiled at his new hand. 'I thought you'd appreciate that today. If I hadn't, we'd end up ridin' twenty or thirty miles today just to find and run in the *remuda*. When we first started the ranch, I fenced off about three sections for horses, then one section just for the horses that we're using. That way they've got room enough, and I did it so the crick runs through all of it, so they always have food and water. But when we want horses, we know where they are.'

'Saves a batch o' ridin' all right,' Trevor agreed. 'You see the rider on the hill?'

Alton whirled around, looking a complete circle, then back at Trevor. Trevor had not turned in the saddle, but continued the way they had been riding. Alton said, 'Who? Where?'

Without looking that way, Trevor said, 'That ridge over to our right. There was a lone rider there a minute ago. He stopped when just his head an' shoulders was above the top o' the hill, an' he saw us. Then he turned the other way.'

'Now who would that be?'

'Somebody watchin' your horses for you, maybe? Your fence been messed with any?'

Alton nodded. His lips tightened. 'It gets cut on a regular basis, but the horses haven't been run off. I chalk it up to Scythe hands. If they want to ride somewhere and there's a fence there, they just cut it and ride through.'

'You ever call 'em on it?'

'No. I've never caught them doing it. I don't suppose I would if I saw them. It's not a big enough deal to start a fight over. Especially when they have a dozen hands and I don't. I figure if I can keep from having a confrontation long enough, the problem will take care of itself.'

'Most problems don't do that. I always figgered if someone wanted what was mine, I'd best stand up to him sooner instead o' later. Win or lose, he'd know he had a fight on his hands to get it.'

Alton didn't answer. After they'd ridden a way, Trevor asked, 'Anybody other than the Scythe outfit get upset at you fencin' the county?'

'Oh, yeah. And a couple guys have refused to ride for me, even when they needed work, because I got fences. If you have any fences, part of what every hand has to do is fix fence.'

'I ain't too keen on that, neither.'

'I don't know anybody that likes to. But it saves a lot of time and ridin'. The day'll come when the whole county'll be fenced, and they'll have surveyors come out and mark out the lines of the edge of everybody's range, and nobody's cattle will even mix with anyone else's.'

'Well, if that ever happens, I hope I ain't around to see it.'

'You will be, unless you get killed first. It ain't that far off. The county's gettin' too filled up with people. When you get too many people, you gotta have fences to keep 'em apart. It'll get just like it is back east, only the places will always be bigger, I 'spect. But it'll come to where everyone has to have a deed to all the land he uses. Then the law will deal with all these questions.'

'I'll move on when that happens.'

'If you have anyplace left to move to, that's any different.'

'There's always more room out west.'

'Not always. The county out west is fillin' up too. That's what's got the Scythe outfit up in arms. It ain't just me they don't like. It's progress and change. It's all us smaller ranchers, and the homesteaders. We all lay claim to a chunk o' land. Then we homestead the part of it with water, and prove up on it. Then we got the government behind our claim to it. Then we buy other chunks next to us, that already been proved up on. Then, first thing you know, everybody starts fencin' the land they got legal title to. Then the Scythe can't run their cows where they always did. Or they can't get 'em from where they winter to the summer range, 'cause there's other people's land in between, and it's all fenced off. I doubt they got legal title to much more land than I do. I know they do to some awful good land, and they got some real good water rights, but most o' what they graze ain't rightly theirs. They just been usin' it a long time, so they figure it oughta be theirs, even if it ain't.'

'Are they buyin' up homesteads too?'

'Sure. Buyin' 'em up or runnin' people off of 'em.'

Trevor nodded off to their left. 'There's the horses.'

'Yup. Looks like they're all pretty much together. We can run 'em all in, or you can try to look 'em over and cut out the ones you want out here.'

Trevor studied the horse herd,

grazing on a slope of lush grass. He kept looking around uneasily, watching for further sign of the rider he suspected was following and watching them. 'It'd be easier to run 'em all in, most likely.'

'I think so,' Alton agreed.

They moved around the herd and started them moving towards the home ranch. By mid-morning they were all in the biggest of the corrals behind the barn.

'Fine lookin' herd o' horses,' Trevor admired.

Alton's pride showed in his face. 'The best,' he agreed.

'I think I'll take that big buckskin stud, if he's broke. He's too old for me to break right away if he ain't.'

'He ain't,' Alton lamented. 'I gotta get him outa the herd, though. He's been the main stud in the herd for three years. He'll be breedin' back his colts if I don't get 'im outa there. I don't need a bunch o' knotheads showin' up in the herd. I think we'll just cut him out separate, an' I'll trade 'im off for a different stud.'

Trevor nodded. 'Makes sense. That bay gelding looks good, and the pinto mare, the sorrel 'n white one, an' maybe that big roan mare.'

'You got a good eye,' Alton admired. 'I think you just picked the best three in the string. They're all broke, but they ain't been used for a year and a half, at least.'

'They'll shape up pretty fast, then.'

Alton nodded. 'We'll keep 'em in the small horse pasture and turn the rest out, except for an extra team. Those two Belgians are the best hayin' team. We'd just as well start usin' 'em on the wagon instead o' the team in the barn. Then they'll be more ready to work when we start hayin'.'

They separated the horses they wanted kept, and drove the rest back into the big horse pasture. Trevor kept the roan mare in and turned the rest of his, including his own horse, out into the small horse pasture. At Alton's orders, he hitched the team of Belgians to the buckboard and drove them down the road a mile and back again. They were a little feisty at first, but settled into the harness quickly. By the time he was back at the house, they were handling well.

He put the team away and saddled the mare he had kept for his own string. She bucked half-heartedly for a little while when he first stepped into the saddle, then responded well to his directions. He ran her around in the corral for a little bit, turning her in tight circles at a dead run, first one direction, then the other. Alton watched approvingly from the top rail of the fence.

Trevor reined up in front of him. 'She is one fine horse,' he exulted. 'She can turn on a dime and leave six cents change layin' there.'

Alton nodded. 'She's a good cow-horse. You can rope off of her, real well. That geldin' you picked ain't never been roped off of, though. The pinto has, but not a lot. They've all worked cows some, though. I got my horse saddled up. We'd best be gettin' out an' checkin' them cows.'

Trevor nodded. They went to the house and ate lunch. Twice during the meal Trevor had to bite his tongue to keep from saying anything when Lavina began berating Leah. As soon as they were finished eating, he and Alton rode out.

There were several new calves, but no cows were having problems, and no sign that anything had been disturbed. It was fully dark by the time they got back to the barn. Supper made Trevor wish he had camped and eaten jerky and hardtack. Lavina was merciless in her constant barrage of criticism and ridicule of both Leah and Stuart. Halfway through the meal she swatted Leah's hand. 'That's no way to hold a fork. It's not a pitchfork. You don't have to spend your whole life acting like you've never been taught anything. If you want to be a slob, go eat in the barn.'

'OK, I will!' Leah yelled. She grabbed her plate and ran sobbing out the door.

Trevor could hold his peace no longer. He stood, picking up his own plate and silverware. 'I guess I was holdin' my fork 'bout the same way she was,' he said. 'I'll just go on out an' eat in the barn too.'

Lavina gasped and stared at him open-mouthed. Stuart jumped up from the table, grabbing his own plate. 'Me too!' he said, darting for the door.

Trevor and Stuart caught up with Leah about twenty feet from the house. Instead of going clear to the barn, she had walked away from the porch and sat down on the ground. She was holding her plate in her lap, staring off into the night.

The full moon gave a soft half-light glow to the evening. Stuart sat down beside Leah. 'Do you know what Trevor done, Lee,' he gloated. 'He went an' tol' Ma that he was holdin' his fork just like you was, so he'd better go eat in the barn too. Then he got up an' walked out with his plate. So I did too.'

Leah looked at Trevor, then back at Stuart. 'You shouldn't have done that,' she said softly. 'Now Mama will be mad at both of you, and she'll blame me for it.'

'She rides you pretty hard, don't she?' Trevor ventured.

Leah nodded. 'I guess she just doesn't like me. I try really hard, but nothing I do is ever good enough. I know I'm clumsy and I'm a brat and I'm stupid, but I try.'

Trevor shook his head. 'No, you're not,' he disagreed. 'You're not at all clumsy. You move around as graceful as a deer, and you're as bright an' pretty as a new dollar. I 'spect your ma just wants you to be plumb perfect.'

'She just hates me,' Leah insisted.

'Me too,' Stuart agreed. 'Maybe she just don't like kids. But Pa does. When he takes us off fishin' in the crick, or ridin' somewheres, or helpin' him with the cows, he's real good to us. He

47

always tells us how proud he is of us, and how good we do, even when we don't do too good.'

'I wish Mama was more like him,' Leah agreed.

At a loss for words, Trevor fell to eating the food from his plate. When they had all finished he said, 'Give me your plates. I'll take 'em all back to the house so you won't have to.'

Leah stood, shaking her head. 'No. I'll take them. If I don't, Mama'll say I was using this as an excuse to get out of helping with the dishes. You too, Stuart. Come on.'

4

'There ain't no way we'll be able to check cows today if we do that.'

Alton Huxford sighed. 'Yeah. I know. And I don't like that either. But I got a real uneasy feelin'. I got to go into town. We need too many supplies. Ma an' the kids got to go too. And I just got a real uneasy feelin' that we might run into trouble in town. I'd just feel a whole lot better if you was with us.'

'What if whoever's watchin' the place decides it's a good time to run off some o' the horses, or help hisself to some o' the calves?'

Alton studied the rim of hills surrounding the valley from under the brim of his hat. 'Well, I guess that's a chance we'll have to take. Anyway, there ain't no way the two of us can watch everything all the time.'

Trevor nodded his reluctant agreement. 'I 'spect that's so.'

Alton continued. 'And if anything gets bothered, I'd soonest it was anything except Vinny and the kids. If somebody decides to bother them, or pick a fight with me over 'em that I can't walk away from, I'd like you there.'

The talk had run on long enough to suit Trevor. 'We best get goin' then, if that's the case. It's almost sun-up. It'll already be dark afore we can get much done in town and get home again.'

Alton nodded. 'I got the team hitched already. I'll drive. You and both kids can ride. That way the kids won't have to sit in the back of that wagon. It beats a body up somethin' awful, ridin' back there all the way to town and back.'

Trevor pondered it a minute, then said, 'Well, you and the missus had just as well get started, then. Me'n the kids'll swing by that one bunch o' heifers an' make sure they ain't none o' them havin' trouble. It's purty much on the way. Then we'll catch up by the time you ain't much more'n halfway to town.'

Without waiting for a response, he turned to the barn to saddle his horse, and two others for Leah and Stuart.

They found two heifers that were having problems calving. Both calves needed to be pulled, but they were able to do so successfully. Both Stuart and Leah proved surprisingly adept at helping. Even so, it took enough time that Alton and Lavina were already in town before they caught up. As they started down the main street of Natrona, Trevor spotted their wagon in front of the Mercantile Store. He headed for it, but was brought up short by a young boy's voice from the sidewalk.

'Weave me awone!'

'Weave me awone,' a second voice mimicked in mocking tones. 'Don't that sound just like some dumb sodbuster's kid?'

A chorus of laughter encouraged the cowboy barring the way, so the ten-year-old boy could not pass on the sidewalk. 'Say something more, kid. What'd you say your name is?'

'Waymond Wobinson,' the boy replied angrily. 'Now weave me awone and get out of my woad.'

The cowboy's answer was drowned out by the guffaws of the crowd that was beginning to assemble in front of the saloon. As the laughter died down, Trevor could hear the cowboy again. 'And tell me, does Waymond Wobinson wike to hunt wabbits and wide wace horses? I mean, howses?'

Another chorus of laughter was interrupted by an angry homesteader, striding along the board sidewalk. 'Hey! What'dya think you're doin'?'

Silence fell across the group of spectators, but the one doing the teasing only grinned a little wider. 'Well, lookee here. Here's Waymond

Wobinson's daddy. I bet he's come to wescue his wittle Waymond from the bad man.'

The homesteader's eyes flashed fire. 'Leave the boy alone. He can't help the way he talks, but he's a lot better off with a tongue that don't work quite right than a brain that don't work at all.'

The grin left the cowboy's face. As it did, Trevor spotted two others moving stealthily towards the homesteader from outside his range of vision. He slid off his horse and handed the reins to Stuart. 'You two stay here,' he ordered. 'Hold my horse, and stay out of the way.'

He started across the street, moving at an angle to approach the two before they could reach the homesteader. With one corner of his mind he followed the conversation.

'You sayin' my brain don't work,' the cowboy asked.

The homesteader showed no intention of backing down. 'Any man that

53

picks on a kid either ain't got a brain or is too yellow to pick on a grown man. Now leave the kid alone, or you'll have to crawl back to the Scythe outfit and tell Pashenka you got spanked by a real man.'

The two men approaching the homesteader from behind quietly drew their guns. One looked at the other, and waved him away. By motions, he instructed the other to put his gun away and simply grab the homesteader, so their friend could do as he wished unthreatened. Both men holstered their guns.

'You better back them words or run like a scared rabbit, I mean wabbit,' the cowboy confronting the homesteader said, cocking his fist to swing.

The homesteader in turn raised his own fists, drawing his right back to begin a swing of his own. One of the two behind him reached for it, then froze as he felt a gun barrel against the side of his neck.

Trevor spoke very softly. 'You two

boys just put your hands down and back off. Your friend called a man out. Now let's just see if he's man enough to back up his words. Just be sure you boys don't let your hands get anywhere near those guns, or I'll drop you in your tracks.'

The homesteader looked over his shoulder, realizing for the first time he had been set up. He looked back at his antagonist. The cowboy had a look of stunned surprise on his face. The homesteader's jaw clenched. His eyes narrowed. The cowboy raised both hands up in front of him, palms facing the homesteader.

The tone of his voice took on an almost pleading note. 'Now we was just funnin' you, Robinson, we didn't really mean nothin' — '

His words were cut off in mid-sentence by the homesteader's fist slamming into his mouth. A fountain of blood sprayed in all directions. He was knocked back two steps by the force of the blow. Before he could catch his balance, another fist caught him on the right jaw. It landed with the sound of a club. His eyes glazed momentarily. Before they cleared, a barrage of blows pummelled his face and body. He staggered backward, trying desperately to keep his feet.

The homesteader stepped into a right that carried the full weight of his body, backed by the muscle of countless hours behind a plough. It connected with the point of the cowboy's chin. It picked him bodily from his feet to land, spread-eagled in the dust of the street.

With no hesitation, he whirled to the two who had been sneaking up behind him. Both men looked back and forth from him to the gun in Trevor's hand, held unwaveringly on them. They looked at each other, then broke and ran into a space between two stores. The homesteader stood in the street, torn between his desire to pursue and warning bells sounding in his mind.

His mind was made up by Trevor's soft words. 'I wouldn't foller 'em in there, was I you. They'll likely muster up enough courage to stop an' wait fer you. You'd be most apt to get yerself shot.'

The homesteader glared down the empty alleyway then back at Trevor. Trevor holstered his gun and held out his hand. 'My name's Trevor Killian.'

The homesteader relaxed and let out a long breath. He took the extended hand and gripped it tightly. 'Orid Robinson. Thanks for buyin' in. I didn't see the two comin' up behind me. They had me set up good.'

'Why are they workin' that hard to set you up?'

The boy walked up beside the homesteader. Orid reached out an arm and laid it across the boy's shoulders, without taking his eyes from Trevor. ''Cause they're Scythe outfit,' he said simply. 'I got a good homestead. Bottom land along the crick. They been tryin' one thing and another to run me off for the past two years. Who do you ride for?'

'Huxford,' Trevor said. 'They try pickin' on your family afore?'

'Not mine, but they used that to get Ole Swenson mad enough to fight. They started hasslin' his girl. She was about fourteen or fifteen, I guess. They made Ole mad enough to pull a gun on 'em, then Kelby killed him.'

'Who's Kelby?'

'Gunfighter. Works for Scythe. Ole didn't have a ghost of a chance against him. He just waited till Ole pulled his gun, then shot 'im right between the eyes.'

'The marshal didn't do nothin' about it?'

A voice from behind Trevor startled him. 'The marshal couldn't do anything about it. Ole drew first. It was a clear case of self-defence, even if it was carefully set up. There were over a dozen witnesses, and they all said the same thing.'

Trevor sized up the newcomer. He appeared to be in his mid-thirties. He stood easily six foot tall, well muscled, with an air of quiet authority. His eyes were such a pale blue they were almost colourless. Trevor had the uneasy feeling those eyes could penetrate clear to his soul. A badge hung loosely on the front of his shirt.

The easy dismissal of the incident rankled Trevor. He said, 'And where was the marshal when they were hassling a young girl?'

Fire flashed briefly behind the bland blue of the marshal's eyes. His expression did not change. 'The marshal can't be everywhere at once.'

Trevor was unwilling to let the matter drop. 'I noticed that a while ago here, when Robinson was being set up for three men to beat him senseless. I didn't see the marshal around then, either.'

The flash of fire in the marshal's eyes was stronger, but was quickly subdued again. With the same expressionless face he asked, 'You tryin' to ask somethin'?'

Trevor's bluntness surprised him. 'Yup. I'm askin' if you make it a practice to be somewheres else when the Scythe outfit's settin' somebody up.'

It was Trevor's turn to be surprised. There was no flash of resentment, no trace of reaction in the lawman's eyes. Instead he appeared almost amused. 'You do get right to the point, don't you? I like that. I hate folks that beat around the bush and ain't never got guts enough to say what's on their mind. The answer is, 'No'. I don't take orders from Pashenka, or any of his boys. I don't ride a circle around 'em. And if they cross the line so I can nail 'em, within the boundaries of the law, I will do it so quick they'll wonder what happened to 'em. But I can't break the law to enforce the right. Even when I want to. And I can't be everywhere at the same time. I just keep doin' the best I can, and waitin' for my chance.'

Robinson spoke up. 'He's tellin' you it straight, Trevor. He's the only man in the county that's ever backed Kelby down, an' I seen 'im do it. He ain't no friend o' the Scythe outfit.'

The marshal smiled tightly. 'I had the edge,' he admitted. 'Even Kelby ain't anxious to draw against a double-barrelled Greener.'

Trevor nodded and again thrust his hand forward. 'That's good enough fer me,' he said. 'I'm Trevor Killian. I ride for H-X.'

The marshal took the hand at once, shaking it firmly and warmly. 'I'm Dave Grimm. Town marshal. Deputy Sheriff, too, but that's just to keep folks from thinkin' I can only enforce the law in town. I didn't know Huxford had any hands any more.'

'Just me,' Trevor said without volunteering any extra information.

The marshal clearly wanted to ask more, but decided against it. Trevor turned back to the homesteader. 'The Scythe tryin' to run all you homesteaders out?'

Robinson nodded. 'Gettin' worse all the time. Sometimes they offer to buy folks out, and sometimes even offer a fair price. But mostly they just keep lookin' for any excuse they can find to scare 'em off, or beat 'em up, or kill 'em.'

'How many have they run off?'

Robinson thought about it for a long moment. 'Probably a dozen.'

Trevor turned back to the marshal. 'You tellin' me that an outfit can run off a dozen different folks from their land, an' you can't find nothin' to do about it?'

The marshal shrugged. 'Nothing I can prove. Not so far, anyway.'

Robinson thrust himself back into the exchange. 'That ain't countin' the half-dozen that's been killed. Or four different guys that just plumb disappeared.'

The implied accusations began to rile the marshal. His jaw clenched. His eyebrows lowered over narrowed eyes. 'I ain't exactly done nothin',' he protested. 'I ran two o' Pashenka's hired guns outa the county. We hanged one for two o' the killin's. But I can't be everywhere at once. You boys has got to protect yourselves, mostly.'

'I thought that's what the law was for,' Robinson protested.

Grimm responded instantly. 'Nope. It ain't never what the law's for. There ain't no way the law can protect anyone, unless you got two lawmen protectin' every person — one to be protectin' while the other one's sleepin'.'

'Then what good's the law?'

'The law's there to punish people after they already break the law. If somebody kills you, then it's my job to find out who did it and why. It's my job to see he's brought to trial. Then it's up to the judge. If the judge orders 'im hanged, it's my job to do it. Whether I agree with the judge or not. That's what the law's for.'

'Then who's supposed to protect us?'

'The only one that can protect you is you yourselves. That's why you got the right to pack a gun. You got the right to work together and guard each other's places. You got the right to do whatever you need to do to protect yourselves. Aside from breaking the law, of course.'

Trevor looked thoughtful. 'I've heard tell they's marshals in a couple places that ain't lettin' folks pack guns in their town at all.'

Grimm snorted. 'There are. They're starry-eyed dreamers, or else somebody blowed half their brains out already and they ain't noticed. The only thing you can ever accomplish by ordering people not to pack guns is to take the guns away from the people that try to obey the laws. They're not the problem. The troublemakers don't pay any attention to the law anyway, so they'll go ahead and pack their guns. They'll just hide them under their shirts till they're ready to use them, and you can't search everybody in town every two hours to make sure nobody's got a gun hid on him. Then when the troublemakers want to, they can haul out their guns and be real sure that nobody can stop them o' doin' anything they want to, 'cause that pigheaded marshal that thinks he's the guardian o' the world has took the guns away from the good people.'

Trevor grinned in spite of himself at the long and impassioned speech of the lawman. 'You're about the first lawman I've run into that talks like he's got a head on 'im,' he remarked.

Grimm took a long breath. 'I'll take that as a compliment. You boys stay outa trouble.'

He turned on his heel and walked away. Trevor turned back to Robinson. 'Do the small ranchers and the homesteaders talk to each other?'

Robinson nodded. 'They're sociable. The only one that don't neighbour none is Scythe, then on north the Bar-None and the Gallows Ranch. They all three work together some, and they all keep tryin' to gobble up the little guys. The rest o' the county gets along pretty good.'

Trevor nodded. He held out his hand again. 'Been good talkin' to you. I gotta get the kids on down to where the boss and his missus are.'

Robinson took his hand and shook it. 'You're welcome to drop around sometimes. Our place is the third one down the crick from the H-X. The one with the rock fence around the house.'

'Where'd you find enough rocks in Wyoming to build a fence with?' Trevor asked.

He could still hear Robinson chuckling as he took the reins from Stuart and mounted his horse.

'Wow!' Stuart breathed when they were away from the homesteader. 'You kept them there guys from beatin' him up! But why'd you let those two get away. Ray's dad woulda whipped both of 'em, if they'da stayed there!'

'I 'spect he would,' Trevor agreed. 'He's a good man with his fists. But those two knew it too. The only way to keep 'em there woulda been to shoot 'em.'

'So why didn't you shoot 'em? They're just Scythe hands anyhow.'

Trevor jerked his horse to a halt and glared at the boy. 'Because they're people, Stu. Even if they ride for Pashenka, they're people. I'll face 'em down when I have a chance. I'll kill 'em if I have to. But I won't never kill nobody unless I ain't got a choice. You don't never kill another human bein' if you got any choice. You understand?'

Stuart stared at his saddle horn and squirmed in the saddle. 'I guess. I didn't really mean it, nohow. I just hate anyone that works for the Scythe. They're all dumb.'

Trevor kicked his horse into motion, and neither Stuart nor Leah said any more.

5

'Looks like two of 'em watchin' us today.'

Trevor's words were soft, but they jerked Alton upright in his saddle as if he had been struck. He jerked his head around, sweeping his eyes across the tops of the hills. 'Two? Where are they?'

Trevor did not move his head, or change the pace of his horse. 'They're 'bout a quarter mile off, over to the right. I saw 'em 'bout a mile from the house. Then I spotted 'em again a minute ago. Looks like they're shadowin' us, stayin' outa sight.'

'Why are they doing that? Why do they just keep watching us that way?'

'Oh, I 'spect it's just to let us see 'em, time to time. That way we stay nervous. If we're nervous enough, maybe we'll do somethin' dumb, an' give 'em an excuse to come an' run us outa the county.'

'If that's what they're trying to do, why don't they just run us off? There's just me and you. There ain't no way we can stand up against the dozen or so hands the Scythe could send over here. They could shoot us, or run us off, burn my place, do whatever they want. Who's goin' to stop 'em?'

'The law.'

'The law? Do you really think Grimm could stand up to 'em any more than we could?'

'Oh, it ain't just Grimm. The law ain't never just one man. The county's gettin' civilized. If the Scythe does somethin' out in the open enough to get folks riled, or to get the attention of the US Marshal's office, or even the sheriff, then they'll have to answer fer it. Once that happens, it'll go all the way to the governor's office, if it don't get settled. Since Wyoming got to be a territory on its own, the governor's real anxious to bring in law an' order.

'Specially since they're startin' to talk about bein' a state. If there's a clear-cut case of a big outfit bustin' the law, he'll hear about it. Then he can even call in the army, if it don't get took care of. Pashenka's gotta be smart enough to know that. Naw, the only way he can get away with takin' your place is to try to get you to do somethin' that gives him an excuse.'

As they topped a small rise, they came into view of the herd of calving cattle. Alton pointed. 'There's a couple new calves. They look fine.'

'Yup. There's another ol' girl over there fixin' to have one.'

'I can't believe how smooth the calving's comin'. We ain't hardly had a problem.'

'We got one now. That old girl over there's lost hers.'

Following his point, Alton spotted a cow nearly a quarter of a mile away. She was separated from the rest of the herd. She stood above an indistinguishable lump of colour on the ground.

Around her four coyotes were ranged. 'Coyotes are after it,' Alton observed. 'Maybe it ain't dead.'

'Dead or not, she ain't gonna let 'em have it,' Trevor approved. 'Let's give 'er a hand.'

As he spoke, he pulled his carbine from its scabbard and levered a shell into the chamber. Alton followed suit, and the two men galloped towards the cow. Too distracted at defending her dead offspring from the encroaching predators, she did not see their approach.

The two galloped to within a hundred yards of the scene. As they swung their horses crossways and pulled them to a stop, one of the coyotes darted in to try to grab the dead calf. The cow whirled and caught him deftly with a horn, sending him airborne to land, sprawling and yelping, in a clump of sage.

Even as the cow started to turn back, another coyote had taken advantage of her distraction to rush in and grab the carcass of the dead calf. The besieging predators, like the cow, were too busy even to notice the approach of the two riders. The bark of Trevor's rifle changed the fact abruptly.

At the first shot, the coyote grabbing the calf dropped without a sound. At almost the same time his body hit the ground, the cow's horn hooked under him, sending his already dead body cartwheeling into the air. A second shot a split-second later, from Alton's rifle, sent a second coyote in a whirling circle of pain and surprise, before he, too, collapsed in death.

The sounds of the rifles obviously reached the animals as the second coyote dropped. Both remaining coyotes and the cow jerked as if controlled by some single, hidden string. Their heads shot up. Their ears went forward. They turned to look in the riders' direction.

In the same instant, the two surviving coyotes shot away from the cow, jumping and dodging in headlong flight. The speed of their reaction caused Trevor's second shot to kick up dirt right at the heels of one of them.

Alton didn't bother firing again. Trevor levered another shell into the chamber and fired once more, leading one of the coyotes by at least four body lengths. In spite of the lead, the thirty-thirty slug kicked up dirt well behind it. Both animals disappeared over the top of the hill.

'Well, we got two out of four,' Alton said, sliding his rifle back into its scabbard.

Trevor paused to reload the magazine on his ownrifle before replacing it as well. 'Shoulda had three,' he lamented. 'I didn't think they'd have time to react quite that quick.'

'They're a quick animal,' Alton admired.

'Pesky too,' Trevor agreed. 'They'da had that calf in spite of the ol' cow protectin' it in another few minutes, an' nothin' she coulda done about it.'

'She sent that one a-flyin' though.'

Trevor chuckled in shared appreciation of the memory. 'She did that. That's the one I missed with my second shot. He'll be good'n sore for a few days, even if I did miss 'im.'

Trevor's never-resting eyes caught movement from their right. 'We got company,' he said curtly.

Alton whirled to see what he was talking about. Two riders were slowly herding a cow with a calf into the herd of H-X cows.

Alton's voice betrayed his sudden concern. 'Now what are they doing?' he said.

'I dunno,' Trevor said slowly, 'but I sure don't like the looks of it. Let's check it out. But watch yourself. I got a bad feelin' about this.'

They rode to intercept the odd procession. As they neared, it became apparent the cow being driven carried the Scythe brand. A few rods closer and Trevor stiffened in the saddle. 'That calf's branded,' he said to the rancher.

'Why would they brand that little a

calf already? It ain't over a week old, looks like.'

'Ten to one it ain't wearin' a Scythe,' Trevor gritted.

'What? What do you mean?'

Trevor didn't respond. He tapped his horse with his spurs, sending it into a long lope to intercept the Scythe riders. Alton did the same, tagging along some fifty feet behind his hand.

'Hey!' Trevor hailed the riders. 'Whatd'ya think you're doin'?'

The two riders reined in. They sat their horses, waiting his approach. Glancing briefly at the cow and calf, Trevor's fears and suspicions were instantly verified. The cow did, in fact, wear the Scythe brand. Her calf, less than a week old, carried the H-X brand, freshly burned into its thin hide.

One of the riders looked grim. The other grinned wickedly. 'Well now, what does it look like we're doin'?' he replied. 'We're hazin' along this here cow that you boys tried to steal the calf off of.'

'We don't brand calves that young,' Trevor protested. 'What're you tryin' to pull?'

'Your funeral, cowboy,' the other replied. 'We just got ourselves some evidence here that you boys ain't nothin' but rustlers an' calf stealers. We just caught you, red-handed, runnin' a long-rope on Scythe livestock.'

Alton had caught up with his hand just in time to hear the last of the conversation. He looked at the cow and calf. The colour drained from his face. He swallowed hard. His voice almost squeaked as he replied. 'You can't pull something like that! Nobody in this county would believe that! You branded that calf yourselves, with my brand, just to try to make it look like I did it!'

The other's grin broadened. 'Did we now?' he taunted. 'You boys is lookin' at your ticket outa the county. Or your hangin'. There ain't no law that'll hold the Scythe responsible for hangin' cow thieves. 'Specially when we got the evidence right here. Right, Shorty?'

The grim-faced rider nodded his agreement. He responded to the conversation between his partner and Huxford, but his eyes never left Trevor. 'That's a fact, Guy,' he agreed. 'You can't argue with evidence like this.'

Trevor and Alton exchanged looks. Guy reached for his gun as he said, 'So I guess you boys better throw down your guns an' get off them horses.'

Before his gun could clear leather, however, he found himself staring down the barrel of Trevor's Colt .45. He had not even seen the cowboy draw. He froze, still gripping his gun, half out of its holster.

'Lift it out real slow,' Trevor drawled. His voice was so soft it was barely audible. The hard flat steel of his blue eyes bored through Guy. There was a whisper of death in his voice as he continued, 'An' drop it in the dirt.'

Guy eyed him coldly for a long moment, clearly judging his chances. He decided on a smart choice. He lifted the gun slowly and dropped it.

Trevor shifted the gun to the other cowboy. 'Now yours too.'

The grim-faced companion of the gunman did likewise. Trevor spoke again. 'Now both of you do the same with the rifles.'

When they had complied, glaring at Trevor, he continued. 'Now you boys get off of H-X land. You can pick up your guns later at the marshal's office.'

Guy struggled visibly for a moment. He glanced involuntarily at his horse's ears. It was obvious he had been told about the other day, when Trevor shot the tip from Hank's horse's ear to end his indecision and speed his departure. 'If you run me off like you did Hank 'n Windy, it'll be the last thing you ever do,' he threatened.

'We'll see,' Trevor said, just as softly. 'But if you try anything except leavin', it'll be the last thing you do.'

Guy swallowed hard. He glanced at his partner. 'C'mon, Shorty,' he said.

Clamping his jaw he lifted the reins

and whirled his mount. He looked at Trevor over his shoulder. 'It ain't gonna do you any good, anyhow,' he blustered. 'You're just puttin' off the inevitable. We'll be back. An' we'll have the marshal with us, too. There ain't no way you're gettin' outa bein' branded cattle thieves.'

With that he jammed the spurs to his horse's sides. The startled animal leapt forward. Shorty followed suit and the two disappeared in a cloud of dust.

Trevor holstered his gun slowly, thoughtfully. Alton inhaled a great gulp of air. He spoke; his voice contained a plaintive note. 'Now what're we gonna do? They'll just bring the marshal an' a bunch o' hands back. We can't get rid o' the brand they put on that calf. They got us over a barrel, Trevor. We're set up as pretty as you please, and there ain't nothin' we can do about it.'

His eyes mirrored the death of a dream. His whole life was wrapped up in this piece of land and herd of cattle. Now it was about to be wrested from him by a clever plot of devious men. He could think of nothing to stop it. The only question still unanswered in Alton's mind was whether to stick around and try to fight the frame-up, and maybe end up hanged, or gather his family and what possessions he could and flee the county. Either way, he had just as well be dead.

6

Trevor studied the fading cloud of dust left by the departing Scythe hands. He pursed his lips thoughtfully.

Alton sagged in the saddle. His shoulders drooped, and his hands lay limp on the pommel of his saddle. His voice reflected the utter despair his posture pictured. 'We're whipped, Trevor,' he said. 'We're boxed into a corner, whipped and hog-tied. We're probably gonna hang. An' there ain't a thing we can do about it.'

'The devil there ain't,' Trevor gritted. 'Rope that calf.'

'What?'

'Rope that calf. Hang on to 'im. I'll be right back.'

He whirled his horse and rode off at a gallop. Frowning, Alton watched his hand ride away. He took in a deep breath and shrugged his shoulders.

Then he unfastened his lariat and shook out a loop. He nudged his horse towards the freshly-branded calf as he started whirling the loop. The horse responded at once. As they approached, the calf turned and ran. The horse knew his business well. He paced the small calf, positioning himself for the easiest cast of the rope for his rider. Alton's loop sailed true, settling over the calf's head. As it did, the horse set his feet, sliding to an abrupt stop.

The calf hit the end of the rope and was hauled up short. The tether spun him around, facing the horse, with the other end of the rope dallied around Alton's saddle horn. The horse backed up as he needed to, to keep the rope taut. The cow tossed her head and bellowed. She walked a circle around her calf and the rider, tossing her head in anger. From time to time she advanced to smell her calf and to assure herself it was all right, but made no effort to charge the horse. Alton relaxed in the saddle, watching Trevor.

Trevor had ridden across the hillside to another cow and calf, That calf was also less than a week old. He, too, shook out a loop and roped the calf. Then he turned his horse and started back towards Alton. The calf pulled against the rope, to no avail. The horse hardly noticed the resistance, pulling the smaller animal along. When the calf resisted too strongly, it was simply pulled from its feet and dragged. When it regained its feet it slid along with all four feet braced, then tried to run off to one side. Again it hit the end of the rope, and was dragged unceremoniously along behind Trevor's horse.

The calf's mother ran along behind. Her tail was up at an awkward angle. Her ears were as far forward as they would flex. Her head was up. She bellowed her rage at horse and rider. Long drools of slobber trailed from her mouth to blow away in the ceaseless wind. From time to time she tried to approach her calf, but the rope kept dragging it along too rapidly for her to be allowed time to check on it.

As Trevor approached Alton, he called out. 'Get a stick and scoop up some o' that ol' cow's droppin's.'

'What?'

'I said, get a stick and scoop up some o' that of cow's droppin's. She's mad as a hornet, and she's asprayin' manure all over. Scoop up some of it.'

'Why?'

'Ain't you never mothered up a calf from a dead cow to a cow what lost her calf?'

'Well, yeah, but what's that got to do with anything?'

'We're gonna switch calves.'

'What?'

'Don't you never get tired o' sayin' 'What'? We can't get rid o' the brand them boys put on their calf, but we can switch calves, an' put that calf on your cow, and give one o' your calves to their cow, an' then they ain't got no evidence no more.'

Alton sat with his mouth open, trying to digest the orders his hand was giving.

Slowly the light dawned, and he grinned. 'By jing, it just might work!' he cried.

He straightened in the saddle; his shoulders went back and the slouch melted away from his posture as if by magic. He nudged his horse, guiding it to drag the calf he had roped over to where the other calf's mother was prancing back and forth. He leapt from his horse and grabbed a stick from the ground. He walked to a fresh pile of cow manure close to the calf his horse was holding tethered on the lariat. The calf's mother ranged back and forth in a half-circle, tossing her head and blatting angrily. 'Just keep an eye on both o' them cows,' he told Trevor. 'I ain't anxious to take a ride on either one o' their horns.'

Using the stick, he kept scooping up droppings from the other calf's mother, smearing it along the calf's back. He continued until he had almost coated the calf's back with the other cow's droppings.

'Now do the same with this calf, but with the other cow's droppings,' Trevor called.

'Well, pull 'im over there by where the other cow dropped a pile, then,' Alton replied. 'I ain't gonna haul it over here to 'im on this stick.'

'Use a different stick, so you don't mix the scent,' Trevor advised.

Dropping the stick, Alton picked up a different one. He repeated the procedure, smearing the droppings of the other cow all over the back of the second calf.

'Now let's see if we got good enough cuttin' horses to haze this calf an' the Scythe cow back over to their range, so they'll both mother up with the wrong cow afore either one of 'em finds her own calf again.'

They urged their horses forward, releasing the tension from both lariats. The calves both quickly shucked out of the loops. Each calf began at once to look for its mother.

Both Alton and Trevor quickly

recoiled their lariats and moved to begin herding the calves. Alton called, 'You take the unbranded one an' the Scythe cow. I'll try to keep the other two here with this bunch, so the calf won't follow you.'

The calves still understood which cow was each one's mother, and continually tried to break around the rider to get back to that cow. The cows kept smelling the calves, obviously confused by the mingling of the scents. Trevor managed to get between the unbranded calf and its mother, moving it and the Scythe cow slowly away from the other pair. Alton moved in between, keeping either member of that duo from following.

Trevor's horse figured out the game at once. His ears perked up. His head stretched forward, low to the ground. His front legs were spread apart, ready to dodge in either direction as he had need. Trevor let the reins hang limp, allowing the horse to do all the work. Every move either cow or calf made, the horse seemed to anticipate a split-second earlier. When either animal broke to try to move around him, he was already moving to cut it off, sending it back.

After the horse had moved the cow and calf a quarter mile from the other pair, it began to be an easier task. Trevor shook out his lariat again. Using several coils of it as a whip, he lashed out with it and stung the cow on the rump. She humped her back and began to run. Trevor yelled at the top of his voice. The calf stopped trying to dodge around him to get back to the other cow, and ran for the relative safety of the Scythe cow's side. Within minutes, cow and calf were moving along, side by side, as if they belonged together.

After Trevor had moved the pair at a good pace for a mile and a half, he eased up and gave them time to stop and rest. The calf ran to the cow, trying at once to nurse. The cow eyed the calf suspiciously, backing in a circle away from it, smelling it and tossing her head. She looked around in vain for a different calf that smelled more convincingly like her own.

The calf was hungry and persistent. He had used up a great deal of nourishment, first on the end of the lariat, then being hazed away from the herd. Finally the cow stopped and allowed it to begin to nurse. Trevor let out a long sigh and began to relax. 'It's gonna work,' he exulted. 'After that calf gets one good bellyful o' her milk, he'll start to smell like hers for real. There ain't nobody gonna prove it ain't her calf after that.'

He gave them several minutes to allow the calf to fill its belly. Then he started them moving again. After he had them almost three miles from the herd of H-X cattle, he wheeled his horse and galloped back to rejoin his employer.

As he loped into view, he saw the branded calf nursing at the side of the H-X cow. The cow stood, head lowered, chewing her cud as if she hadn't a care in the world. Alton grinned at him as he rode up. 'By jing, it worked!' he crowed. 'It took a while. They fussed around some. The ol' cow went back over with the others and tried to find a different calf she could claim, but then she come back. By then this calf was hungry enough he didn't care who Momma was, as long as she'd let 'im suck. She finally did. She'll claim 'im, now.'

Trevor nodded. 'Just in time, too, I'd say.'

Alton looked up to see what Trevor was looking at. A party of men had just topped the hill, riding hard. A spot of light flashed, as the sun reflected from the badge on the shirt of one of the riders. 'Now how do you suppose they went an' got the marshal, and got back that fast?'

'Must've had 'im on the way already,' Trevor observed. 'They wasn't takin' no chances on not makin' things stick. If we hadn't acted plumb fast, they'da had us.'

They sat their saddles, waiting until

the group approached. Dave Grimm, the marshal from Natrona, was accompanied by Shorty and Guy, along with Windy and Hank, the two other Scythe hands Trevor had run off the ranch previously. Alton greeted the lawman. 'Howdy, Marshal. Little ways outa town, ain't you?'

'Howdy, Alton. Not by choice. These boys sorta hauled me out here. Somethin' about catchin' you red-handed stealin' Scythe calves.'

'That right?' Alton responded, glaring at the Scythe hands. 'Well, they're lyin', but that ain't uncommon. If they had an ounce of honest blood, they wouldn't be ridin' for Pashenka.'

'Are you callin' me a liar?' Guy challenged.

Trevor's voice was soft as he intruded into the conversation, but its answer to the challenge was unmistakable.

Guy's face flushed. His hand dropped to inches above the gun butt protruding from his holster. Trevor wondered idly whether it was an extra gun he already had in his saddle-bag, or one he had secured from one of the others.

The stern voice of the marshal intervened. 'Hold it! We ain't gonna have any gunplay. You two both just back off, and let's get this matter settled.'

He turned to the four hands of the Scythe ranch. 'You boys see this calf around that you say has an H-X brand on it?'

Three of the hands lifted the reins of their horses and moved towards the herd of cows, feeding along the side hill. Guy stayed as he was, glaring at Trevor. Trevor returned the gaze steadily, without expression. The marshal nudged his horse and moved between the two. His voice was gruff as he told Guy, 'Go find that calf, if you got somethin' you want me to see.'

Guy jerked his horse's reins and rode off at a trot. One of the other Scythe hands yelled, 'He's over here. I found 'im.'

The others rode quickly to the motioning cowboy. He was pointing to the young calf, bearing the unmistakably fresh brand of the H-X. The marshal turned to Huxford. 'Brandin' 'em awful young, ain't you Alton?'

Alton shrugged. His face was expressionless. 'Yeah, it looks like. Did you brand him, Trevor?'

Trevor's face was just as empty of expression. 'Nope. I ain't even carryin' an iron, or even a cinch ring to brand with.' He turned to his boss. 'You 'spect someone else's brandin' our calves fer us, just to be sure we don't lose none?'

Alton almost smiled. 'Well, could be, I s'pose. That sure would be neighbourly, now wouldn't it?'

Guy Kelby sneered. 'Don't get smart! That there calf belongs to a Scythe cow. You put your brand on a Scythe calf, and you know it.'

As if in answer, the cow whose calf had been switched trotted to the branded calf. She was obviously still uneasy from the activities that had resulted in her calf being roped and dragged around. She smelled the calf and nuzzled it, then began licking its face. The calf moved alongside the cow and began to nurse.

Alton could not resist commenting. 'Well now, that there sure looks like an H-X cow to me that calf's a-suckin'. What makes you think it ain't?'

Guy barked at the others. 'He just branded one of his own too. Look around, boys. There's gotta be another calf that size with the H-X on it.'

Shorty was staring at the calf in obvious confusion. 'Naw, that there's the right calf,' he said. 'He's got that white spot like a half moon on his left ear an' that little chunk outa the tail. That's the same calf we . . . uh . . . that is . . . uh . . . the one what we saw before.'

The marshal spoke up. 'I don't even see a Scythe cow in the herd.'

The four Scythe hands looked around as if to contradict him, but they were as unable to spot any of their own brand. It was Guy who spoke up again. 'There was. I was here, earlier, chasin' down one of our cows with a calf. I seen that Scythe cow, right here. Then this gun hand o' Huxford's threw down on me'n Shorty an' made us throw our guns in the dirt.'

The marshal's doubt crept into his voice. 'You mean there was one lone Scythe cow, at least four miles away from all the other Scythe cows, and you boys just happened to notice it.'

Guy looked uncertain for a minute, but recovered quickly. 'Well, the fact is, we was trackin' it. It looked like someone was drivin' the cow an' calf, so we thought we'd oughta foller along the trail of it an' see what was goin' on. Ain't that a fact, Shorty?'

Shorty looked quickly back and forth from the marshal to Guy. His brow was furrowed deeply with the unaccustomed effort of thinking. Then his face lit up. 'Uh, yeah! That's right. Just like Guy said. Yeah. There sure was a Scythe cow over here, all right. An' he sure did throw down on us all right. That there fella did. Just made us throw our guns right down in the dirt, he did.'

Windy entered the conversation. 'This is not the first experience of our ranch hands with this hired gunman,' he informed. 'Myself and Hank have already been victims of his all too readiness to involve gunplay in the sooth and transpondence of normal ranching business and duties. Why he forced us at the gunpoint of his rifle to throw our own firearms in the very dirt and ride away — '

The marshal looked at Alton and cut off Windy's verbiage. 'Is any of that true, Alton?'

Alton almost smiled again. 'Oh, they was here, all right. They was rantin' an' ravin' about some cow o' theirs. Then they tried to get tough, so Trevor just made 'em leave their guns. Oh, the guns are over there on that little knoll, if you boys want 'em. They're still lyin' right where you dropped 'em.'

Grimm cut in. 'What about their

cow? Did you see one?'

It was Trevor who spoke up. 'Well, yeah, matter o' fact, we did find that cow. Since they was so all-fired het up about it, I figured it must be a purty important cow, so I hazed her an' her calf back over to their grass. Seemed the least I could do to be a good neighbour. I left 'er two or three miles over north, there. I sure didn't see no brand on the calf, though.'

The four Scythe hands stared at each other in mutual confusion. Grimm waited for some response from them, but none was forthcoming. Finally Trevor spoke up again. 'If these boys is so anxious fer you to see that cow, I 'spect you can foller my tracks easy enough. I hazed her off between them two big ol' rock spires stickin' up yonder. 'Bout a mile an' a half past 'em is the end o' H-X land. Why don't you boys head over that way an' show the marshal that real important cow o' yours. Then you work real hard to stay over there, off o' H-X land. If I see any o' you on this outfit's land again, I'm most likely to figger you're lookin' fer trouble.'

He glared directly at Guy as he continued. 'If that happens, I ain't like to give you a chance to toss your guns away again.'

Guy Kelby glared at Trevor as if to burn holes through him. His mouth pressed into a thin, white line; the muscles at the hinge of his jaw bunched. His hand inched closer to his gun butt. Finally he said, 'I'm goin' after my guns. Then we'll go find that cow. I'm plumb anxious to see how you wiped that brand off'n it.'

He and Shorty rode to the knoll where they had dropped their guns. Shorty dismounted and handed Guy's guns to him, then picked up his own and remounted. Then the two spurred their horses into a lope towards the direction Trevor had indicated. The other two Scythe hands followed wordlessly. The marshal looked at Alton and Trevor. 'I seem to be missin' somethin' here,' he observed. 'I ain't sure what, but I'll be interested in seein' what happens when we track down that cow. Meantime, you boys best watch your back.'

He touched his hat to them and rode off in pursuit of the other four. Alton and Trevor watched them ride out of sight. Then Alton said, 'I'd sure like to see their faces when they find their cow with an unbranded calf a-suckin'.'

Trevor smiled in spite of himself. 'Yeah, but they'll be back,' he warned.

The chill up Alton's back assured him his hired hand was right.

7

'I'd love to know what they found.'

Trevor smiled wryly at Huxford. 'I know what they found. They found their cow, with a calf a-suckin' what didn't have no brand at all. What I'd like to know is how they explained to the marshal why they'd dragged him all the way out there to see it. I'd sure like to've seen their faces.'

Alton Huxford sighed. 'I'd give a whole lot more to know what they've got up their sleeve next.'

Trevor's face was grim as he stared at the sagebrush-covered hills. 'Me too. I 'spect maybe I could take a day an' ride into town. I could talk to Grimm, an' maybe nose around town a while. Might be able to pick up some gossip that'd give us some idea what they're likely plannin' next.'

Alton thought it over for several

minutes as he finished lacing the leather thong he was using to repair his stirrup strap. Finally he said, 'Yeah, you do that. But watch yourself. Tomorrow's as good as any.'

At supper, later, Alton mentioned the plan to Lavina. 'Trevor's goin' to town tomorrow, Vinny. You got anything you need 'im to pick up?'

Lavina looked back and forth between the two men. 'Is something wrong?'

Alton shook his head quickly. 'No, no. We'd just sorta like to see how the wind's a-blowin', and what the marshal thinks o' the whole situation.'

Lavina's nervous look moved back and forth between the two men until she was satisfied. Then her face grew thoughtful. 'I could use a couple sides of bacon and a bolt of cloth. But I don't know how to describe the cloth I want. Maybe you couldn't carry both on horseback anyway.'

'Can I go with him, Momma?' Leah asked. Her hopeful eyes were wide with pleading. 'I could spend some time with Sophie and Sally. I haven't seen them in such an awfully long time. Please, Momma?'

Lavina's response was instant. 'What? Go all the way to town with just you and Trevor? Why the whole county'd be talking.'

Alton held up his hand. 'Oh, now Vinny,' he soothed. 'They wouldn't no such thing. There ain't nothin' in the world wrong with her ridin' to town with Trevor.'

'Then who's going to do her chores?' Lavina protested. 'She doesn't do enough work around here to even know she's alive most days, and now you want to let her go gallivanting off all over the county all the time. How is she ever going to learn to be responsible if she starts doing that?'

Alton was unmoved. 'Aw, she can use a day away from the chores.' He turned and addressed the girl. 'Just you be ready whenever Trevor says he'll be back at Sophie's to pick you up to come home.'

'I will, Papa,' Leah beamed. 'Thank you, Papa.' Then, as an afterthought, 'and Momma.'

Lavina sighed. 'Well, then, since you're going, you can stop at Webster's and pick up a bolt of that lavender calico that we were looking at. I can use it for new dresses for both of us, and a new tablecloth as well. Maybe even some curtains for the kitchen windows.'

'Oh, Momma,' Leah enthused. 'That would be pretty. Tablecloth and curtains the same material! And our dresses, too! You could make Papa and Stu shirts out of it, too. Then we'd all look like we were rolled out of the same big machine!'

Lavina scowled. 'Are you making fun of me, young lady?'

Leah's smile vanished. Even so, a mischievous quirk toyed at the corners of her mouth. 'Oh, no, Momma. I just thought it was funny. You'd just have to be careful not to bend over, though. Somebody would think you were the table, because you'd be bigger than it. You might get something hot set on top of you.'

Lavina's face turned scarlet. 'Young lady, you do not talk to me that way! I will not have you making fun of my weight, or anything else about me. Just for that, you may not go to town at all.'

Leah's face fell. Once again, Alton stepped in. 'Now, Vinny. She didn't mean nothin' by it. She was just funnin', that's all. She didn't mean no disrespect.' Trevor struggled to hide his smile. Thinking it best to beat a hasty exit, he stood to leave. As he scooted past Leah, heading for the door, she muttered, 'Yes I did!' so only he could hear.

The next morning, just before sun-up, he emerged from the barn with his and Leah's horses saddled. The soft light of kerosene lamps glowed in the kitchen windows. He tied the horses to the corral fence and walked up the hill to the house. The rest of the family, except Lavina, were already assembled at the breakfast table. He noted that Leah was dressed for riding. She bubbled, 'See, I'm all ready to go.'

Unwilling to rekindle the previous night's argument, Trevor declined to comment. Instead he mumbled, 'Good morning,' and fell to eating at once. Lavina bustled about the kitchen. She slammed pans and skillets with somewhat more noise than usual, but offered no greeting and no response. Her face was frozen into a pout of displeasure. She looked at nobody, busying herself away from the table. When he finished eating and stood, Leah silently followed him to the door. Neither spoke until they were well clear of the house, down the hill nearly to the barn. Then Trevor said, 'I wasn't none too sure you'd get to go.'

'Me neither,' Leah admitted. 'But I'd have snuck out and run my horse to catch up with you if I'd had to. If I had to be here another day, listening to her without a break, I think I'd go crazy.'

They mounted their horses and rode

quickly from the yard. As they toiled up a long hill, they stopped to let the horses rest. 'Your Ma does ride you some, but you know that's 'cause she cares, don't you?'

Leah snorted. 'She doesn't care about anything but stuffing her face and getting her way and making me cry.'

Trevor frowned. 'No, I don't think so. I think your ma's really pretty proud of you. I think she's so proud of you, she just wants you to be plumb perfect. She ain't too good at sayin' so. What she does is notice anything that ain't quite perfect, an' holler at you about it.'

'She hollers, all right,' Leah agreed. 'She hollers like some fat old cow with her tail caught in a gate. Only all she hollers is, 'Leah this,' and 'Leah that.' I hate her!'

'Aw, now, you don't hate 'er. You just hate 'er hollerin' at you.'

'I hate her! I wish she'd fall in the wash boiler when she's boiling wash water.' Leah giggled unexpectedly.

'Except she's so big and fat she'd just splash all the water out and wouldn't even get burnt.'

Trevor frowned and shook his head, fishing for words that wouldn't come. Finally he said, 'Well, I think you're one swell girl. I wish you was my kid.'

'I don't want to be your kid,' Leah said quickly. 'I want to be your girl.'

Trevor's head jerked up. Leah was busily staring at one of her saddle strings. She continued without looking at him. 'I want to be your girl. Your woman. I'm old enough. You can take me away from here, then I wouldn't ever have to see that place again, and I wouldn't ever have to hear her tell me how stupid I am, or how bad I am, or how lazy I am, or how fat I am, or what a brat I am or, or, or . . . '

She turned towards Trevor and reached out her arms to him. Unaware of what else to do, he held out his arms. She rushed into his arms and clung to him, sobbing into his shoulder. He held her silently, suddenly painfully aware that she was not a child. It was a woman's body that pressed against him. He fought the feelings that welled up unsought within him.

After she had sobbed herself out, she pushed slowly away from him. 'I, I'm sorry,' she stammered, wiping her face with the sleeve of her dress. 'I know you couldn't never be interested in somebody as dumb and ugly as me, but I like you anyway. You treat me like you think I'm a real person, and you don't butt in when I'm telling something, and you even listen to me.'

'Of course I listen to you,' Trevor protested. 'You got a good, quick head on you. You just gotta use it to think about how good you are, not makin' yourself think them things your ma says when she's upset.'

'She's always upset,' Leah gritted. 'She hates me. And I hate her, too.' Stepping back into the saddle, she spurred her horse into a lope.

Trevor leapt into the saddle and set out in pursuit. 'Prob'ly hadn't oughta run 'im too much,' he called. 'It's a long way to town.'

Leah reined in and waited for him to catch up. By the time he did, her eyes were dry, but her expression was far from cheerful. Little by little, as they rode along, Trevor lightened the mood. By the time they reached the halfway point to town, she was chatting merrily. She hardly stopped for breath until they reached Natrona.

He escorted Leah to the Wilsons' house. He remained on his horse. 'You'd best make sure they're home,' he said. 'It's past eight o'clock already.'

No sooner had he said it than the door flew open and a fifteen-year-old girl with flaming pigtails burst out into the yard. 'Leah!' she called. 'How'd you get to come to town?'

'Trevor brought me,' Leah grinned in response. 'I can stay all day.'

Sophie beamed with excitement. 'Oh, that's wonderful! Come on. We'll put your horses in the stable out back and feed them some grain. Then we'll walk over and see if Sally's busy today . . . '

Trevor did not wait to be dismissed. He let Sophie take the reins of his horse. He strode to the marshal's office. David Grimm was leafing through papers at his desk as Trevor walked in. 'Well, if it isn't the notorious calf rustler from that hotbed of crime at the H-X,' he commented drily.

Trevor held up both hands and grinned. 'Come to turn myself in an' throw myself on the mercy o' the court,' he said.

Grimm grunted. 'I thought maybe you came to fetch me out on some all-day wild goose chase after phantom brands that disappear right off the sides of calves.'

Trevor's grin widened. 'That's the Scythe's angle. I don't deal with phantom brands. I deal mostly just with phantom Indian war parties.'

Grimm abandoned the levity and asked, 'What was goin' on out there?'

Trevor shrugged, unsure how much to tell. Finally he said, 'Oh, just a

110

sorry-legged try at framin' me'n Alton, so they could try to run us outa the county. We just managed to outsmart 'em, is all.'

'What'd they do, put your brand on one o' their own calves?'

Trevor hesitated again. 'Well, I guess 'bout all I can say is if there was any calf branded, they did it.'

Grimm nodded. 'How'd you get your own cow to claim it?'

Trevor held both hands out in front of him. 'I didn't say we did nothin' at all.'

Grimm waved his hand. 'I ain't tryin' to get you to admit nothin'. I know what Pashenka's boys are tryin' to do. I was just plumb tickled you turned the tables on 'em. But they're determined. Sooner or later they'll back you boys into a corner.'

Trevor nodded grimly. 'I 'spect,' he agreed. 'I ain't shyin' away from that a bit. I just wanta be sure they ain't got no leg to stand on with the law when it happens. I can hold my own with

Pashenka's boys.'

The marshal looked doubtful. 'There's quite a few of 'em.'

'There's quite a lot of me,' Trevor said with a grin. 'An' Alton ain't no slouch.'

The marshal nodded, but his look of doubt remained. 'Watch yourselves.'

'Plan to,' Trevor replied. 'You ain't heard what they're plannin' next?'

The marshal shook his head. 'Nope. I heard they're havin' troubles calvin' their heifers. They got quite a bunch o' first-calf heifers this year, an' they got all they can do takin' care o' them, right now. Once calving's all done, though, they'll be back to barkin' at you boys' heels.'

Trevor nodded and shifted his hat a little lower on his head. 'Well, let 'em bark,' he said. 'I'll pick me up some turpentine.'

The marshal laughed at the unexpected response. 'You might find their tails a little harder to turpentine than most stray dogs.'

'Yeah, I bet they'd sure howl, though,' Trevor said as he walked out the door.

He walked down the street to the saloon. He ordered a beer, then put a lunch together from the things laid out on the bar. He sat down and ate, visiting idly with the patrons who came and went. He quickly learned the whole county was abuzz with the efforts of the Scythe Ranch to run off the smaller outfits. He heard several rumours of his own prowess, from those who did not know him, that made him smile. He learned nothing of substance, except that the homesteaders and smaller ranchers were growing desperate in their fear of Pashenka.

8

Trevor stepped out of the saloon into the afternoon sun and let his eyes adjust. He had walked no more than ten steps when a woman's voice brought him up short. 'I said, 'No, thank you',' the voice said with strong emphasis.

Trevor stopped and turned. A young woman was trying to walk down the far sidewalk. A cowboy had her way blocked. His hat was in his hand, but his face was hard. Unsure what to make of the situation, Trevor started across the street.

The cowboy spoke. 'Now, that there's a word I ain't used to hearin' from the ladies,' he said. 'Especially purty ladies. I just plumb got my heart set on takin' you to that dance tonight, and I just ain't gonna take no fer an answer.'

The young woman glared at him.

Her face was red with anger, but the flush served only to accentuate her beauty. Reddish-blonde hair framed her face with gentle curls below her bonnet. Even in the shadow of the bonnet's brim, her brilliant blue eyes flashed fire. Fierce anger put a sharp edge of steel on her words. 'You will take no for an answer, and you will get out of my way and let me pass,' she said.

The cowboy only laughed. As he approached, Trevor recognized him as one of the Scythe hands. 'Hank,' he told himself as he approached.

Hank said, 'Oh, come on, sweetheart. You know you can't hardly resist me. How 'bout you just give me a kiss.'

The cowboy did not see her fist coming. Instead of the slap he may have expected, her right fist crashed into his jaw with astonishing strength. He took an abrupt step backward. The shock and surprise on his face turned to fury. 'Why you stuck up, high an' mighty strumpet — slug me will you?'

He reached out and grabbed the

woman's arm. Trevor neither spoke nor slowed his approach. From a step and a half away, he swung his right fist. He propelled himself and the streaking fist forward to contact the extended chin of the furious cowboy. It connected with a sodden thud that sounded like a wooden club striking a fence post. Hank's eyes rolled back. His knees buckled. He toppled backward and landed on the sidewalk. His knees remained bent. One arm dangled loosely over the edge of the side-walk. The other lay at his side. He did not move.

The woman stared dazedly at him for an instant, then whirled to face Trevor. He laughed at the expression of startled wonder on her face. He swept off his hat. 'You prob'ly oughta close your mouth,' he said softly. 'Flies is sorta bad this year.'

Her mouth snapped shut. She opened it to speak, then closed it silently. She looked back at the unconscious cowboy. Trevor said, 'You pack quite a punch.'

Her eyes darted back to his. She was suddenly struck with the ridiculous nature of his statement and she giggled. 'That was quite a punch,' she agreed, 'but I'm sorry to say it wasn't mine. I'm afraid mine only succeeded in making him angry.'

'He was sorta hot under the collar,' Trevor agreed.

She reached out and touched his arm. 'Thank you for rescuing me. He really was becoming quite obnoxious.'

'My pleasure,' Trevor responded. 'I sorta owed 'im one anyway. Oh, my name's Trevor Killian. I work for the H-X.'

'Oh,' the woman responded. 'I have heard of you. My name is Millie Ralston. You have made quite a name for yourself. A name not too much appreciated among the Scythe sympathizers, I'm afraid.'

'Fond of me already, huh?'

He delighted in the sound of her giggle. 'Not exactly. The gossip around town is that you have given them a little more than they could handle lately. They aren't very used to losing, you know.'

'How do you fit in?'

She smiled. 'You come right to the point, don't you?'

'Well, I ain't gonna waste any time standin' here on the street talkin' to someone that thinks the Scythe outfit is right about anythin'.'

Her smile faded. A look of bitterness crept around the corners of her mouth. 'You will find no love for Pashenka or any of his bullies in me,' she said.

He smiled in an effort to soften her expression. 'Well, then, in that case, any enemy of the Scythe is a friend of mine. May I see you safely home?'

Fire flashed briefly in her eyes at the suggestion. Then her eyes were drawn again to the inert form on the sidewalk. She glanced around at the silent crowd that had assembled. Softly she said, 'Thank you. I think I would like that.

We seem to be becoming a spectacle here.'

He stepped on to the sidewalk and offered her his arm. With an almost imperceptible flicker of surprise at the gallant gesture, she laid her hand in the crook of his elbow and they began to walk. The crowd on the sidewalk moved aside silently to make room for them. Neither spoke until she had guided him to a small house two blocks from the main street.

'This is where my mother and I live,' she said. 'Won't you stay and have a drink of something? Mother usually has some tea made. She leaves it in the cellar so it's nice and cool.'

'Now that sounds real invitin',' Trevor responded, 'but I wouldn't wanta impose on you none.'

'Oh please,' she insisted. 'It is no imposition. But mother is at work, so it might be best if we sit here on the porch to drink it. I'll go get us each a glass.'

Three wooden chairs were ranged

along the front of the house. Trevor sat on one and waited until she returned with two glasses of tea. 'I took the liberty of putting a little honey in yours,' she said. 'I hope you like it that way.'

'Never tried it,' Trevor responded. 'I don't get things like honey too often.' They visited over the glass of tea as long as Trevor thought he could stretch it. Then he said, 'I got some things to buy, then I got to head back to the ranch.'

Disappointment was obvious on Millie's face. 'Oh, must you? I was hoping when Mother comes home you'd have some supper with us. That would seem to be a more proper expression of gratitude for rescuing me than a glass of tea.'

Trevor smiled ruefully. 'That's an offer I couldn't refuse any other time. Fact is, I brung the boss's daughter into town with me, to see some o' her friends.'

'Leah?' she asked. The surprise was

evident in her voice.

He nodded. 'If'n we ain't home by dark or thereabouts, they'll worry some.'

'Oh, how thoughtful of you,' Millie responded. Her voice ended up in the air, as if she wanted to say something further, then thought better of it.

Trevor picked up on the indication. 'But I'd sure like to take you up on the invitation the next time I get a chance to come to town.'

Her smile told him all he needed to hear. Later he couldn't even remember exactly what she'd said, but he couldn't get the smile out of his mind. If he hadn't been thinking about that smile so intently, the voice from the street wouldn't have caught him so much by surprise.

'That's far enough, Killian!'

The voice jerked him from the pleasure of his memory. His eyes darted to the middle of the street. The cowboy he had recently knocked out stood there, feet spread apart. He had a firm grip on the handle of his pistol. His growling voice dripped anger and hatred. 'You sucker-punched me, right in front of a woman, you two-bit drifter. I'm gonna kill you right where you stand for it.'

As he spoke he drew his revolver from its holster. Trevor's own hand streaked towards his gun. In a motion too swift to see, his gun swept up and spat a streak of fire towards the furious cowboy.

The other man's gun came to bear briefly on Trevor, but wavered from the impact of Trevor's bullet striking its owner's body. He tried to bring it back in line with his intended target, but another slug followed the first into his body in such rapid succession he was unable to do so. He frowned stupidly, as though trying to understand what was happening. Then, without another word, he dropped to his knees. His gun slipped from his fingers. He crumpled forward in a twisted heap. His face pointed straight down into the dust of the street, and he made no effort to turn it. There was no life left in him, and so no need to move out of the dirt to breathe.

At the sound of the shots, the marshal lunged from the door of his office, gun in hand. He stood on the sidewalk, fifteen feet from Trevor and looked over the situation. 'What's goin' on, Killian?' he asked.

Trevor sighed. He ejected the spent cartridges from his pistol and replaced them with shells from his belt. He reholstered his gun. Only then did he turn to face the marshal. 'He's one o' Pashenka's boys. He was givin' a woman a bad time, wouldn't let 'er git past 'im on the walk. When he grabbed 'er, I hung one on 'im. Cold-cocked 'im. Then I took 'er home.'

'Who was she?' Grimm interrupted.

'Millie Ralston.'

'How'd you know her?'

'I didn't, till just then. Anyway, I walked 'er home. When I come back, he yelled at me. Already had his gun half outa the holster. Said he was gonna kill me fer bustin' 'im in front o' Millie. Didn't give me no choice at all.'

Grimm looked around at the inevitable crowd. 'Did any of you see it?'

'Just like he said, Dave,' a businessman replied. 'I saw the whole thing. I saw Hank out here in the street, and I wondered what he was waiting for. Then I heard him yell at Killian here. He didn't even give him a chance to say, 'No thank you'. He just said he was going to kill him, and pulled his gun. If Killian wasn't faster'n blazes he'd be dead.'

Grimm nodded. 'I'd already heard about you sluggin' him,' he said. 'I knew there was gonna be hell to pay for it. There still will, most likely, once Pashenka hears about it.'

Just then Leah rushed up. 'I heard shooting! Oh, Trevor, are you all right?'

'I'm fine,' Trevor said shortly. 'But you'd best get our horses. We'll pick up the stuff your ma wanted from the mercantile store an' head fer home. It's gonna push us to make it by dark now.'

Leah's face betrayed a hundred more questions she wanted to ask, but she pushed them down and turned to obey. When she returned, they both hitched their horses in front of the mercantile store and went inside.

'Aren't you Trevor Killian?'

Trevor whirled to face the woman wearing the leather apron. 'Seems everyone in town knows that already,' he responded.

She smiled. Her voice was deep and rich. Her face was lined, but pleasant. 'You have made quite a name for yourself. I'm afraid everyone knows who you are.' Trevor looked at her more closely. Something hauntingly familiar about her eluded him. Her eyes were deep blue. The reddish-blonde of her hair was streaked with grey. Lines of sun and care were etched deeply into the skin of her face, but she stood tall and straight. Her shoulders were broad for a woman. Her gaze spoke of a deep reservoir of iron strength.

'Well,' he said, 'I guess that gives you the advantage. I don't know who you are.'

She smiled, softening the hard lines of her face. 'I'm Matilda Ralston. Millie's mother. Thank you for intervening on her behalf. I'm sorry it required you to kill a man. But if someone had to die, I thank God it was one of the Scythe's hands.'

Trevor digested the glut of information in that one statement silently. Her resemblance to Millie accounted for the strange familiarity that had mystified him. But how did she already know about his intervening to save Millie from the cowboy's unwanted advances? Why did she take the death of a man so easily in her stride? Why did she hate the Scythe ranch so virulently? He said, 'I take it the Scythe Ranch ain't your favourite outfit.'

Her lips instantly compressed into a thin, hard line. Her eyes went flat and empty. Her words suddenly had a hard edge absent moments before. 'I have no love for that ranch or the animal who runs it. Thank you for getting rid of one of them, at least. If you wish some target practice, I would encourage you to regard their ranch as a prairie dog town, and shoot as many of them as possible.'

Taken aback by the vehemence of her diatribe, Trevor said, 'Well, I don't know that I'd go that far, but I 'spect they're a den o' rattlesnakes all right enough.'

Matilda Ralston's mouth was compressed so tightly the corners were white with the pressure. Her eyes were distant. With an obvious effort, she forced her mind away from her thoughts and back to the present. 'Well, that's neither here nor there, is it?' she said. She took a deep breath. 'I'm sorry to let my feelings show so much. What can I help you with?'

'Well, Leah wants a bolt o' some stuff 'er ma was lookin' at a while back.'

'Oh, yes. The lavender calico. She wants the entire bolt?'

Leah spoke up. 'Yes. She wants to make clothes for everybody and the windows and the table, so that we all look like the fabric got caught in a whirlwind and wrapped us all up in it, and if she has any left over she will probably make sheets for the bunk-house out of it too.'

Matilda laughed a deep throaty chuckle. 'You don't sound too excited about a dress that matches the curtains.'

Trevor thought it best to head the conversation in a different direction. 'Your daughter gave me a glass of that cold tea you make, with honey in it. I hadn't never drunk none o' that afore.'

'Did you like it?'

'Oh, yes ma'am. It was a real fine drink.'

'Did Millie invite you for supper?'

'Uh, well, yes ma'am, she did. But I sorta had to say no. I gotta get Leah home afore dark, or her folks'll be a-worryin' some.'

'Well, maybe a different time, then?'

'I'd like that a lot. Yes ma'am. I surely would.'

'Well, then, the next time you stop into town you let me know you're here right away, and consider yourself invited for supper that day.'

'Why, thank you ma'am. That's plumb nice o' you. I'll sure do that.'

'Is there anything else you need?'

'Uh, yes ma'am. I need some ammunition. An' I was wonderin', do you have any light oil I can use on my guns?'

'I have the ammunition, but you will need to get the oil at Ben Silverman's General Store. He carries that, and coal oil, and things like that.'

'Fine. We gotta stop over there an' pick up a couple sides o' bacon anyway.'

They charged the material to the H-X, but he paid for his ammunition. Then they walked across to the General Store, got the rest of the things they needed and headed out of town. They were less than half a mile from town when Leah said, 'You like her, don't you?'

'What? Who?'

'Millie Ralston.'

'Whatd'ya mean? I ain't never even met 'er afore today.'

'But you like her, don't you?'

'Well, yeah, I guess maybe I do. She sure is a pretty thing. Smart, too. You shoulda seen her punch that fella. She didn't slap 'im. She just up an' slugged 'im on the jaw. Took 'im back a step, too; it did. Why? Don't you like her?'

Leah's face was a sudden picture of suppressed anger. She did not answer for quite a while. Finally, Trevor pressed the issue. 'Don't you like Millie?'

After a long and heavy silence, she said, 'I don't really know her. I guess she's all right. If you like your women that old.'

She kicked her horse into a trot, moving ahead of Trevor, out of conversational range. Trevor frowned at her back. He spoke more to himself than to his horse. 'Now what's eatin' her?'

Two or three times in the next hour he thought she was using her sleeve to wipe a tear from her cheek, but she did not allow him to catch up, or to ask questions. Every time he urged his horse to a faster pace, she did too, staying about three lengths in front of him. Leah did not speak another word to him on the ride home.

9

'Trevor! Trevor! Help me!'

Trevor looked up from the calf just emerging from the birth canal of the cow. Leah was riding down the small valley as fast as her horse would run.

He stepped away from the cow, as she skidded to a halt. She flew from the saddle and threw herself into his arms. 'Oh, Trevor, don't let him take me!'

Trevor wrapped his arms around her and held her until her violent trembling subsided. 'Let who take you?' he asked.

'Jack. Jack Warden. Oh, Trevor, he scared me!'

'What did he say? What did he do? Where did you see Warden?'

'He rode over there where I was helping with calving. In that next valley, where Daddy had me working. He was real nice at first, and it was really fun to talk to him. He kept telling me how pretty I am, and everything. Then he tried to talk me into running away with him. He said he'd take me to Denver, and buy me anything I wanted, and I could be his girl. When I told him to go away he got mad and he got real mean. He told me he could take me to Denver and I couldn't do anything about it and nobody would ever find us. Then he grabbed me.'

'He grabbed you?'

'I stomped on his foot as hard as I could with my boot heel, and he hollered and let loose, and I jumped on my horse and ran. I thought he was going to catch me.'

Trevor's eyes had gone hard and flat. He looked back the way Leah had come, seeing nothing. He stepped away from her. 'You ride to the house,' he said.

He walked to his horse and stepped into the saddle. He jammed the spurs to the horse's sides. Surprised, the horse leapt forward as if shot from a cannon. In four jumps he was in full

133

stride, running flat out, his belly seeming almost to skim the top of the low sage brush.

It took less than twenty minutes for him to catch up to Jack Warden. Warden saw him coming, and stopped his own horse. He stepped three or four steps to the side, awaiting Trevor's approach.

Trevor slid to a stop and leapt from his horse. 'Warden, you yellow-bellied idiot!' he fumed. 'What do you think you're tryin' to pull with that girl?'

Warden grinned maliciously. 'What's the matter, Killian? Too stingy to share your private whore?'

'What did you say?'

'You heard me. Whole county knows you been toppin' off the boss's daughter. Huxford ain't got no money to pay you, so he lets you have his daughter instead, way I heard it. I figger you oughta share with the rest of us.'

Trevor's face lost all expression. His eyes were cold and flat, as hard as frozen steel. He spoke softly. 'Warden, there ain't a man alive can say stuff like that about anyone I care about. You better fill your hand or drop the gunbelt and I'll beat you plumb to death.'

Warden's smile was frozen to his face, its mirth not reflected at all in the hard glint of his eyes. 'I was hopin' you'd say that,' he replied.

As he spoke his hand streaked to his gun. It hadn't even cleared leather when Trevor's gun barked. It came free of the holster as Trevor's gun barked the second time. It dropped to the earth as the third shot rang out. Two more bullets found their mark before his dead body had time to collapse.

Trevor stood, breathing hard, watching the lifeless form for a full minute. Then he calmly ejected the spent cartridges from his gun, reloaded, and put it in the holster. Then he mounted his horse and rode back the way he had come.

By the time he got to the house, Leah had already told her story to her parents. They were all waiting for him at the breakfast table.

'Somebody'd oughta ride into town, let the marshal know what happened,' Alton worried.

Calving had been a long month, almost devoid of sleep, with two men, a teenage girl and a young boy trying to do the work of half a dozen hands. They were all dead tired.

'I'll do it,' Trevor offered.

Everybody turned to look at Trevor. It was Lavina who spoke up. 'But you've been up all night, almost every night. You're dead on your feet.'

Trevor shrugged. 'I've had as much sleep as anyone. I'll take a fresh horse. I'll use Socks. He's steady. I kin sorta doze while he's a-goin'.'

'You sure?' Alton asked. 'You could catch a nap first, anyway. A couple hours ain't gonna make much difference.'

Trevor shook his head. 'If I sleep a couple hours, I'll need eight or ten more. Anyway, I thought maybe Kelby'd be in town, waitin' to see if Warden managed to make off with

Leah. I'll be interested in knowin' who else has been told I been foolin' with Leah. If Kelby has, I sorta wanta tell 'im to 'is face that 'e's a liar.'

Alton studied his hired hand carefully. Stuart had fallen asleep at the table, and Alton was having trouble not following his lead. Leah had talked with her parents for a while, then she too had gone to bed.

'Well, do what you think best,' Alton said finally. 'Just watch yourself. They'll be out to get you, you know.'

'Somethin' else I gotta git off my chest first, now that Leah's gone off to bed,' Trevor said.

Alton and Lavina both frowned at him. 'What?' Alton demanded.

Trevor hesitated only an instant. 'I'm sorta surprised Leah didn't go with him.'

'What?!' Alton and Lavina shouted at once.

'I'm plumb surprised she didn't take the chance,' he repeated.

'Why on earth would she do that?'

Lavina demanded.

' 'Cause o' you, Ma'am. You keep ridin' that poor girl every minute o' the day. You tell her she's worthless an' dumb an' lazy an' ugly an' things I wouldn't tell a dog. Then some feller comes along an' tells her how purty she is, an' smart an' wonderful. She'd likely walk off with the devil himself to have that change.'

He hesitated a moment, then plunged ahead before he lost his nerve. 'If you don't let up on her, an' start makin' her feel good about herself, it's just a matter o' time till she goes off with some smooth talkin' ladies' man.'

Lavina's face was a mask of anger that suddenly melted into a wellspring of tears. 'I'm not trying to drive her away,' she wailed. 'I just want her to be good and do right. I want to be proud of her.'

'You can be proud of her,' Trevor insisted. 'She is all them good things. But if you don't start tellin' 'er so, she ain't gonna be here very long. That's all. I said my piece, and I 'spect I'm plumb outa line, but I had to say it. I'll go now.'

Without waiting for an answer, he walked out to catch the horse that would carry him to town. By the time he got to town, he regretted his willingness to open his mouth, and his willingness to volunteer for the trip as well. He did doze in the saddle, but every time he woke with a start, reaching for his gun. He never knew what woke him each time, but by the time he got to town his nerves were on edge.

He stopped first at the Mercantile Store. As he hoped, Millie was there, helping her mother. She beamed as he walked in. 'Trevor! What a pleasant surprise.'

Then her expression changed abruptly as she remembered that the whole county was buzzing about him and Leah. 'Have you heard what they're saying about you and Leah?' she asked.

Trevor nodded. His face was grim.

He was suddenly aware that he had not shaved for two days. His features were drawn and haggard with lack of sleep. 'That ain't the worst,' he said. 'Warden tried to get 'er to run off with him, then he tried to kidnap her when she wouldn't. She's home, an' she's OK.'

Matilda Ralston had walked up to the pair as they talked. She looked first at Trevor then at her daughter. 'She's home?' she asked. 'Somebody said she'd run off with you.'

Trevor nodded. 'She's home,' he said again.

'Is she all right?' Matilda pressed.

Trevor nodded silently again.

Millie stamped her foot. 'Well don't just nod your head! Tell us where the stories started. Did she run off? Was she with someone? What happened?'

Trevor grinned in spite of his fatigue. 'You sure do got a lot o' questions,' he observed. 'You fixin' to write a dime novel or somethin'?'

Fire flashed from Millie's eyes before

she realized he was teasing them. She put her hands on her hips. 'Mister Killian, if you have any hope of that supper I promised you, you had better offer us at least some information in exchange.'

Trevor took a deep breath. His smile faded. 'Well, one o' Pashenka's boys rode out to where she was night calvin' and tried shinin' up to 'er. He tried to get 'er to agree to run off with 'im. She wasn't that dumb. Then he grabbed her, but she stomped on his foot an' got away. She come ridin' over to the next valley where I was night calvin', ridin' hell fer leather. It was just comin' daylight. She told me what happened, so I went an' had a little chat with 'im about it.'

Millie's eyes flashed fire again. 'Who was it?'

'Jack Warden.'

'I knew it! He thinks he's irresistible to women. He probably filled her head so full of lies she didn't know how to say no.'

Matilda interrupted. 'What happened?'

Trevor's eyes were fixed on Millie, even as he answered her mother. 'He wasn't too anxious to apologize. I had to kill 'im.'

Millie gasped. A strange look of triumph passed across Matilda's face, but she covered it up at once. 'Finally! Serves him right,' she said softly.

The response surprised Trevor. He started to ask why she said that, then thought better of it. 'Anyway, Leah's fine. I just rode in to let Grimm know about it.'

Millie laid a hand on Trevor's arm. The hand felt warm and soft against his skin. A glow seemed to radiate from it and spread all the way through his body. He looked into her eyes, and felt suddenly as if he wanted to dive in and lose himself in their liquid depths. She said, 'You must be completely exhausted.'

He nodded. 'I'm some tired all right.'

'Why don't you go over to the house and sleep for a while?' she suggested.

'You can use my bed. I'll be here all day helping Mother.'

The idea was suddenly almost overwhelmingly inviting to Trevor. He felt so utterly exhausted he wasn't sure he could even get to the house. Matilda spoke up. 'We'll take care of your horse, if you just put him in the shed out back. Millie's bedroom is the one on the left. But don't you dare lie down with your boots on!'

Trevor involuntarily looked down at his boots. Then he looked back up at Matilda. With an exaggerated look of wide-eyed innocence he said, 'But I ain't stepped in nothin' all day.'

Matilda swatted at him with the bolt of cloth she held in her hands. He ducked and scurried out of the door. Then he turned and stuck his head back inside. 'Would you sorta spread the word around that Leah's home an' OK?' he asked Millie. 'An' you might add that I'll be plumb happy to visit with anyone that wants to spread any kinda stories about her.'

143

She smiled at him. 'Go get some sleep. The whole county will know what happened and who's spreading the gossip before you wake up.'

She was probably right. He took off his boots at the door. He hung his gunbelt on the post of the bed's headboard and fell across Millie's bed. He inhaled the fragrance of hair on her pillow once, and was asleep before he could remember releasing the breath. When he wakened the sun was moving towards the Big Horn Mountains to the west.

He buckled his gunbelt on, slipped into his boots, and made a hurried visit to the outhouse. Then he walked to the shed and checked on his horse. Socks was munching hay contentedly. His saddle was on a wooden saddle tree, the bridle hung on the saddle horn. He nodded with satisfaction and walked to the Mercantile Store.

'Well, you woke up!' Millie commented brightly as he entered.

He grinned. 'I ain't none too sure

yet. I sorta dropped off kinda quick, I guess.'

'I looked in on you,' she admitted. 'You were sleeping pretty soundly.'

Matilda walked up, then glanced out of the front window before she spoke. Her eyes narrowed, and her lips compressed to a thin white line. Hard lines creased her face around her mouth.

Trevor turned to see the reason for the abrupt change of attitude. Guy Kelby and another rider were passing by in the street. The second horseman was a huge barrel of a man. His ears seemed almost to rest on his shoulders. His hat was pulled low, but no hair whatsoever showed from beneath its band. His clean-shaven face was red and weathered, and wore an expression of arrogant impatience.

'Who's with Kelby?' Trevor asked.

Fire flashed in Matilda's eyes as she answered. 'The Russian,' she said, biting off the words as though it were some fierce invective.

'Alek Pashenka,' Millie explained.

'Scythe Ranch,' Trevor added to the description. 'Be back in a minute.'

'Be careful!' Millie gasped, intuitively knowing where he was going.

Trevor unfastened the strap from his Colt as he stepped through the door. Stepping off the sidewalk he barked, 'Kelby!'

The two men reined in their horses and turned to face him. Pashenka glowered at him without recognition. Mirth played around the corners of Kelby's mouth; it vanished as Trevor spoke. 'Kelby, I thought you might like to know the Huxford girl's home.'

Caution dropped a veil over the gunman's eyes, his face wiped clean of expression. 'Oh?' was all he said.

'Just thought you might like to know that. The two-bit ladies' man that wanted to shine up to 'er ain't that lucky, though. Wasn't Warden one o' your hands?'

Pashenka spoke up for the first time. 'Wasn't?'

'Oh, yeah,' Trevor said with exaggerated unconcern. 'He sorta made the mistake o' thinkin' he could mouth off about a decent girl. He even thought he could lay a hand on her. I 'spect you could probably ride on to H-X land far enough to pick up his body if you don't want the coyotes eatin' it.'

Pashenka's face turned crimson. His heavily-browed eyes glowered from deep within the anger of his face. 'You killed one o' my hands?'

'I wouldn't be braggin' none 'bout hirin' the likes o' him,' Trevor said softly. 'For that matter, I guess the same thing goes for the man beside you. I hear he's been spreadin' some big cock'n bull stories about that girl. That's why I wanted to talk to you, Kelby. I just wanted to tell you to your face that you're a yellow-bellied coward and a liar.'

Kelby's face turned as white as his boss's was red. His hand inched towards his gun. He swallowed hard. His eyes darted quickly to Pashenka, then back to Trevor. He swallowed again. His boss finally intervened.

'You've been a bur under my saddle longer'n any man that's lived,' Pashenka growled. 'If you've an ounce of brains you will leave the county. If I find you anywhere in the county after today, I will kill you like vermin.'

Trevor laughed, sounding much more confident than he felt. 'If you was man enough to do that, I 'spect you'da done it a long time ago,' he taunted. 'Fact is, your days o' runnin' roughshod over this county is just about all done. But if you think you're man enough to kill me, now's as good a time as any.'

The red of Pashenka's face turned almost purple. The veins bulged in the sides of his neck. Kelby's face turned so white even his lips were devoid of colour. Even the ceaseless Wyoming wind seemed to hold its breath, waiting to see what the pair would do.

It was Pashenka who finally broke the spell. 'I'll kill you,' he gritted. 'I'll kill you so you'll know who's doin' it, and we'll see how cocky you are then. You just bought yourself a funeral.'

Trevor forced his grin to widen. 'Well, now, that's real neighbourly of ya,' he said. 'An' here I always figgered I wouldn't be able to afford no funeral.'

Pashenka started twice to say something, but the words caught in his throat. Finally he whirled his horse and jammed his spurs into the animal's sides. The horse squealed in startled pain and then shot forward, carrying his rider back out of town. Kelby looked at the departing back of his boss in disbelief, then back at Trevor. Then he, too, wheeled his horse and rode in pursuit of his employer.

Trevor let the grin fade from his face and heaved a great sigh of relief. Millie and her mother ran from the Mercantile Store. 'Oh, Trevor,' Millie gasped. 'Why ever did you do such a thing? They might have killed you!'

'Yup,' he agreed. ' 'Cept they wasn't quite sure they could.'

Matilda's face wore a strangely

triumphant expression. All she said was, 'You will eat supper with us, won't you, Trevor?'

That was exactly the invitation he was hoping to hear. Among other things it saved him from needing to think about the threats the owner of the Scythe Ranch had made. He was fully aware they were not idle threats.

10

'They want to know what they can do.'

Trevor had no illusions about what agreeing to the request would mean. He had already seen a range war once. He had promised himself then he would never be involved in another. Now he was being asked to be the cause of one.

'If the homesteaders an' the little ranchers organize, Pashenka'll take it as declarin' war,' he explained. 'That'll give 'im all the excuse he needs to come after everyone.'

'There is nothing illegal about organizing to protect their own homes,' Matilda reasoned.

Trevor sighed. 'That's true 'nough. But it still tells Pashenka we're fixin' to fight. He didn't carve a ranch outa Indian county, then hold it against rustlers an' hard winters an' everything else by waitin' fer the fight to come to him. He's tough an' he's smart. He knows if we organize, the only thing that'll keep us from winnin' is to hit first an' hit hard.'

'But if he tried that, wouldn't the marshal be able to step in?' Millie asked.

Trevor was spared the need to answer. Matilda's bitterness was expressed in the snort of derision at her daughter's naïveté. 'Where was the marshal when he killed your father?' she asked.

Trevor waited for some explanation, but none was offered. He said, 'Pashenka killed your husband?'

Trevor was taken aback by the fierce bitterness in the woman's eyes. 'Him and those murdering gunmen Kelby and Warden,' she affirmed.

Trevor looked back and forth from Matilda to Millie, seeking answers to the dozen questions the revelation raised. Finally he simply asked, 'What happened?'

The question was met with a long

silence. Millie studied her hands, twisting them together in her lap. It was Matilda who finally answered. Her voice was soft and low, pregnant with repressed pain. 'It was nearly eleven years ago,' she began. 'We had the prettiest homestead you ever saw. We had water and grass, and a finer home site could not be imagined. It was like a picture in a fancy book.'

She paused and stared into her memories for a long moment, then continued. 'Hiram built a house for us that was far more house than we would need, unless we had half a dozen kids. I know he wanted that many, but after Millie was born we couldn't seem to have any more. We did have one boy, but he died before his first birthday.'

She sighed heavily with the memory, and Trevor thought he was going to have to ask again, but she resumed the story. 'Anyway, Pashenka decided he wanted our place. He offered Hiram money for it. Not enough, but it was something. Hiram laughed at him.

Then Pashenka threatened him, and Hiram ran him off the place.'

A bitter mirth twisted the corners of her mouth momentarily. 'You should have seen it,' she said. 'Hiram had his shotgun, and he forced Pashenka to leave. But Hiram had it loaded with rock salt. As they started to ride out of the yard, he shot Pashenka's horse in the rump. I think he got Pashenka some, too, but most of it hit the horse. The horse absolutely went crazy. He bucked and ran and twisted and did things I have never seen a horse do in my life. But Pashenka actually stayed in the saddle. He was swearing and screaming and hanging on to the saddle horn with both hands, and Hiram was laughing and yelling back at him. Finally the horse just started running, and the last we could see was a dust cloud. I shouldn't wonder that poor horse ran himself to death trying to get away from the awful burning that must have been in his hide.'

Her face softened a little with the

memory of her husband's courage, even though it was obvious she had not approved of taking his anger out on Pashenka's horse instead of him. She looked back at Trevor, remembering the story she was telling.

'He shouldn't have done it. It gave him great satisfaction, but he shouldn't have done it. Pashenka wanted our place too badly, and that gave him all the excuse he needed. It was only two weeks later he hanged Hiram.'

Trevor was stunned. 'Hanged him?'

She nodded grimly. 'Him, Kelby, and Warden. They claimed they had caught him putting our brand on one of his calves. They showed the sheriff a Scythe cow with a calf. The calf had our brand. They claimed they rode up on Hiram just as he was freeing the calf, after he had branded it.'

The words sent a chill down Trevor's back. He remembered a scene of eerie similarity, when Alton Huxford would certainly have been hanged for the same pretended crime, if he had not been there.

'An' folks believed him?'

Millie spoke up. 'Who was going to argue? Nobody else was there. Nobody had the nerve to stand up to Pashenka and his gunmen and call them liars.'

Matilda turned back to him. 'That's why you have to help,' she insisted. 'Nobody else has been able to stand up to Pashenka and survive. There is nobody else the homesteaders will listen to, or rally behind, to organize and resist his determination to dominate the county. Did you go to school?'

Trevor frowned. 'Nope.'

Matilda nodded as if confirming what she had already known. 'If you had, one of the lessons of history you would have learned is the necessity of people standing together. When our county fought free of British rule, in the Revolutionary War, one of the nation's leaders, I think that it was Benjamin Franklin — '

'I've heard of 'im,' Trevor injected.

Matilda nodded. 'I think he is the

one who said, 'If we do not all hang together, we will all be hanged separately'.'

Trevor chuckled softly. 'Good choice o' words, I 'spect.'

'And true of our situation as well,' Matilda pressed. 'If I can get them all to come to a meeting, will you talk to them? Will you help them figure out some system of helping each other, of standing together?'

Trevor held out his hands in a gesture of helplessness. 'What are we goin' to do? We can't just up an' ride on the Scythe an' wage war. If we wait fer him to come to us, he'll hit us one at a time. By the time anyone else gets here to help, it'll be too late.'

Matilda grew animated. 'You can make a system of signals. The Indians used smoke signals in the daytime and fires at night. I've been working on some plans. Millie and I have discussed them at great length. I've even drawn up a map. If a system of fires is prepared at the tops of all the hills I have marked on the map, almost all the homesteaders and small ranchers will be able to see them. If anyone comes under attack, they can light their signal fire, then defend themselves. Those who see the fire can light their own, then go help. In a matter of hours a whole fighting force can be assembled, right where Pashenka is attacking.'

She pulled out a roll of paper and unrolled it on the table. It was a map of the area, drawn with surprising detail. Trevor studied it carefully. Finally he said, 'Well, you know the lay o' the land better'n I do. I ain't been here all that long. But what I know looks like you got it figgered out real fine. It just might work. Provided everybody's watchin' fer the signals at the right time.'

'They will just have to become accustomed to watching for them,' Matilda asserted. 'There is no other way.'

Trevor chewed thoughtfully on a match. 'I s'pose you got it all figgered out how to get 'em all together fer a meetin' too?'

Matilda smiled. 'I have taken the liberty of sending a messenger to as many of them as I could, in one day. I have asked them to assemble at the Lady's Slipper tonight.'

Trevor's eyebrows rose. 'You already called a meetin'?'

Millie laid a hand on his arm. 'We were sure you wouldn't refuse to at least talk to everyone,' she said softly. 'We haven't had anyone to turn to for leadership until you came, and we were afraid we might not have much time. I hope you don't think we were presumptuous.'

Trevor fought the distraction of the glow that spread from the touch of her hand on his arm. The greater struggle was with an entirely unfamiliar feeling of being wanted and sought and manipulated into being a part of strangers' lives. All his life had been a series of rejections, until he had come to consider himself a castoff of society.

Now, suddenly, he was being sought, and being told he was of vital importance to the lives of people he hadn't even known two months ago.

He sought refuge from the confusion of his thoughts. 'I ain't even sure what that there word means,' he mumbled.

Millie smiled, moving her hand to rub his arm softly. The feelings it aroused nearly cost Trevor the last dregs of his concentration. They certainly robbed him of any ability to refuse the request. Millie said, 'I just meant I hope you don't feel like we did something we should have asked about first. You were sleeping, and we didn't want to wait till you woke up. And we didn't know if you would be able to stay in town another day . . . ' she moved the hand back and forth on his arm again, 'even though I was sure hoping you could. Anyway, we just decided to go ahead and call a meeting and hope you'd forgive us if we shouldn't have.'

Trevor looked into the deep blue pools of her eyes. He studied the curls of her reddish-gold hair as it framed the most beautiful face he had ever seen. He swallowed hard. He fought the feelings he sure hoped she wasn't noticing. He stood abruptly and walked away. 'I 'spect we'd just as well talk to 'em,' he said brusquely.

It was just as well he didn't see the tender look in Millie's eyes, or the sudden, fierce flash of triumph in Matilda's.

He was not at all ready, however, to have the two women accompany him to the Lady's Slipper. 'That there's a saloon!' he remonstrated. 'Ladies don't go nowheres near a saloon. Even fer a meetin'!'

'I have every right to attend this meeting,' Matilda insisted, 'and I would attend it if it were held in a whorehouse.'

Millie turned crimson at the word, but Trevor scarcely noticed. 'It ain't noways fittin',' he insisted.

He could just as well have been talking to the wind. In the end the three of them marched together to the Lady's Slipper. When they walked in an instant hush spread from them to engulf the entire bar-room in profound silence. Drinks were suspended halfway between tables and mouths. Words were cut off in mid-syllable. Mouths hung open. A full minute passed in which the entire place seemed frozen in time.

Batch Holmes, owner of the Bar-B-Bar Ranch was first to recover. He set his drink down and rose, extending a hand. 'Well, Mrs Ralston. And Mildred. It is indeed an honour that you two ladies have come to join this meeting.'

He shook hands with the two ladies then turned to the room filled with homesteaders, ranchers and cowhands. 'Boys, these here ladies are two that've lost the most, tryin' to stand up to the Scythe, and by jiminy they got a right to be here for this here meetin'. If there's anyone that don't think so, you come see me.'

Three seconds of silence followed, then a general groundswell of acceptance and agreement began, ending in an easy consensus and welcome for the ladies. Trevor noticed with amusement that nobody continued with their drinks, however. Those who had frozen in place with drinks halfway to their lips set them back down. Cigars and cigarettes were snuffed out and not relit. The whole saloon took on a strange, artificial atmosphere.

Matilda easily and naturally took control of the meeting. She stepped up on the small stage beside the piano where a rare performer sang or danced. 'I sent word to everyone to come tonight, because we have to band together, or Pashenka will run us all out of the county, one by one,' she began.

The meeting lasted scarcely two hours. Trevor marvelled at the way in which all those present accepted Matilda's leadership, his own role that Matilda spelled out to them, and the plan for uniting that she had worked out in advance. They all recognized the shortcomings of the plan, but nobody had a better one to offer. They seemed to be past thinking they could escape the situation without an all-out confrontation with the Scythe. That was especially cemented when three of those present reported that Pashenka had been importing gunmen, and his crew now stood at nearly twenty men, no more than five of whom were legitimate cowboys.

After the meeting three of the ranchers left with Matilda to work on details of the plan. Trevor took advantage of the opportunity to walk home slowly with Millie. They circled the entire town *en route*, revelling in each other's company, laughing at trivial things, stopping to discuss more serious matters earnestly. By the time they reached the house, she had taken hold of his hand as they walked. The feeling her touch radiated through him was like nothing he had ever experienced. He thought that, in spite of the dire threat that hung over his life, he had never been happier.

11

'Where's 'er calf?'

Trevor and Alton both looked around in confusion. The old cow was bawling incessantly. Her udder was swollen out of proportion. Alton put into words what they both knew with the instinct of any cowman. 'Bag's really full. Her calf ain't sucked all day at least.'

'There's another,' Trevor said, pointing.

Alton's eyes followed the direction of Trevor's pointing finger. A hundred yards away another cow, also bearing the unmistakable marks of a nursing cow without a calf, was bawling a constant call to her missing offspring.

'Coyotes get 'em, you 'spect?' Alton wondered aloud.

Trevor shook his head. 'Not likely. They're right in the herd. The coyotes might manage to get one away from the cow if they caught 'em out alone. This close to the herd, though, they'da had half a dozen mad mammas chasing 'em down if they tried. More likely wandered off or died.'

'Well there's another one!' Alton exclaimed.

A third cow, also frantically looking for a missing calf, was racing back and forth along the top of the low rise. Her agitation was telegraphed in every action as well as in the tone of her frantic calls for her missing offspring.

'Well somethin's sure got 'em,' Trevor said softly. 'Let's backtrack one of 'em an' see what we can find.'

It was a difficult chore, trying to backtrack any of the three cows. Their calves had been missing for too long, in the middle of too many other milling, grazing cattle. Finally, on a hunch, Trevor rode away from the herd, riding towards the Scythe ranch.

When he had gone what he estimated a sufficient distance, he began a long slow circle around the area of the herd.

He had not gone two hundred yards when he abruptly reined in. He studied the ground, then began to follow a set of tracks he had crossed.

When he saw his hired hand stop and change directions, Alton lifted his own horse to a lope and joined him. 'Find somethin'?' he called out as soon as he was within voice range.

Trevor did not look up as his employer arrived and reined in. He moved around the side of the gently-sloping hill, first this way and that. Alton folded his hands on the saddle horn and waited.

Trevor spent thirty minutes studying the ground in a large circle. Then he looked at the rancher. His eyes were flat and hard. 'I found somethin',' he affirmed. 'Three riders. They each one roped a calf. Then they musta laid it across their saddle or somethin'. Tracks o' the calves just disappear. Then the three rode back towards the Scythe.'

'How long ago?'

Trevor's face was a study in confusion. 'Not as long as the cows' bags would make ya think,' he said slowly. 'They musta been past due to suck already, afore they snagged 'em. I'd 'spect maybe two, three hours.'

Alton's voice was soft, like the inflexible blade of a sword sheathed in velvet. 'I guess it's time to put a stop to this,' he said. 'Let's go get 'em.'

Trevor frowned. He sat without moving for a long moment. Then he said, 'I'll go get 'em.'

Alton shook his head. 'There's three of 'em.'

Trevor shrugged. 'That's so,' he agreed, 'but that ain't the point. The point is, we got a chance to catch 'em red-handed stealin' your calves. You whip inta town just as fast as you can, without killin' your horse, an' get the marshal. You can guess just about where I'll hit Scythe range, so you won't have no trouble findin' us. I'll track those boys, an' try to have 'em all wrapped up fer ya.'

Alton hesitated for a long moment. Then he said simply, 'You watch yourself.'

He wheeled his horse and kicked him into a long lope, heading towards town. Trevor lifted his own horse to a trot, following the trail the three Scythe riders had left.

As he approached Scythe land he knew he should slow his approach and exercise more caution. At the same time, he felt the urgency to intercept the trio before they had time to match the calves up to Scythe cows. He knew that three of them would take time, even if they had three specific cows in mind. Sorting through the options as he rode, he surmised they probably did. They probably had three cows that had just lost calves. Rather than report the loss to Pashenka and face his anger, they had opted to replace them with H-X calves, still unbranded.

It was only chance that had allowed him and Alton to discover the theft immediately. Any other time, it would have been two or three days before the loss was detected, and it would have been too late to prove whose calves they were. As it was, if he could intercept them before they had opportunity to confuse the animals' scents and get them 'mothered up', it would be obvious to anyone with a modicum of knowledge about cows that they were wrongly matched.

He was less than a mile into Scythe land when he topped a small rise and reined in abruptly. He moved his horse behind a large clump of sage, below the crest of the hill, and studied the layout of the land in front of him.

Less than a thousand yards in front of him, where the next hill started to rise, he could see three distinct, dark shapes against the ground. It was too far to be certain, but he was almost sure it was the calves, still tied, lying on the ground. No other cattle or riders were in sight.

He frowned. 'Must've left 'em there

an' went to round up the cows,' he muttered.

He studied the lay of the land again. By retracing his route a short distance, he could circle around, staying out of sight, and emerge from over the hill, in a grove of aspen trees. That grove ended less than a hundred yards from where the calves lay on the ground. It looked like the ideal approach.

An hour later he slipped quietly through the thick growth of aspens. His horse was tied up twenty feet behind him, well concealed. He nodded with satisfaction. What had only been dark shapes on the ground from his former position were, in fact, the missing animals. He hunkered down where he had a clear view of the hog-tied calves and waited.

He did not have long to wait. He heard them before he could see them. Three cows, bawling, snorting and fighting on the end of three lariats, do not make for a stealthy approach. As they came into sight, Trevor smiled tightly. The three cows, all bearing the Scythe brand, were very obviously devoid of nursing calves. Their udders were so distended they had to be sore. He doubted they would allow their own calves to nurse, let alone strange calves. He guessed the Scythe hands would probably tie the cows so they had no choice. Once the hungry calves filled their bellies a time or two with a cow's milk, the pressure would be relieved from their udders, making them less sore and tender. At the same time, the scent of the mother would begin to mix with the foreign scent of the wrong calf, and she would be likely to claim it.

What they did not count on was interference. Trevor backed quietly into the brush and timber. He mounted his horse and rode as silently as possible to the edge of the trees, where he could once again watch. He wanted to wait just as long as possible to make his move.

It took the three a lot longer than he had expected to secure the cows. It was one thing to keep the three secured with a lariat — that required only one good horse — but with all three horses occupied with holding a cow, none was left to apply a second or third rope to any of the cows. That meant each cow had to be approached on foot by a cowboy using a spare rope. He had to rope one hind leg of the cow, then tie that leg up, forcing her to stand on three legs.

With one leg tied up, the cow could not kick the hungry calf away. If she tried to pick up a hoof to kick, she would fall. At the same time, the lariat around her neck kept her from backing away from the calf. A persistent, hungry calf would succeed in nursing, in spite of the cow's best efforts.

It took the Scythe hands nearly two hours to secure the cows. By the time they finished, they were exhausted. They took time out to sit on the ground and have a cigarette. Then they started to walk towards the calves, still tied up on the ground some fifty yards distant.

Trevor let them get two-thirds of the way there, then rode out of the trees.

'You boys sure do look busy today,' he said in a conversational tone.

The three froze in mid-step, standing as if suddenly struck to stone. Then, as if in a comedy pantomime they turned around slowly, acting in perfect concert, to face the unexpected voice.

Trevor sat his horse almost casually. Across his saddle, his cocked thirty-thirty rested with its barrel pointing directly at them. His finger was on the trigger, but he did not lift it.

'You got somethin' special in mind fer them there H-X calves, or you just lookin' 'em over?' he asked.

The three looked at each other, then back at Trevor. They all swallowed in comic unison. They all turned as if by one impulse to look at the tethered calves, then back to Trevor. Finally, one of them spoke up. 'Uh, them ain't H-X calves. They're Scythe calves. All three of 'em is. The cows, they just went an' got sore an' won't let 'em suck, that's all.'

Trevor smiled tightly. 'It ain't gonna wash, boys,' he said. 'I tracked you all the way here. I know what cows they belong to.'

The three looked at each other again, alarm making their actions begin to take on a jerky, hurried air. Then the spokesman took a deep breath. 'Well, now, that's what you say,' he began. 'Us three, we see it different. One agin' three ain't very good odds, even for someone as fast as they say you are, Killian. I don't think you're dumb enough to try takin' on all three of us.'

Trevor's mind was racing. He did not know any of the three. Two of them appeared to be normal cowhands. The third, who was doing the talking for the trio, had, instead, the look of a gunman. If it came to a shootout, Trevor knew that man had to die first. Even so, he was not at all sure he could lever and fire the carbine fast enough to keep from getting killed. The question was whether they wanted to kill him badly enough to gamble on being the survivor.

Even as he measured his chances, a movement on the hilltop caught his eye. Two riders, their horses in a dead run, topped the hill and started down into the shallow valley they were in. Even at that distance, he recognized his boss and the marshal.

Trying not to show the extent of his relief, he said, 'I don't have to take on all three o' you boys. That there's the marshal's job. He just rode over the hill, yonder.'

Once again acting as if they were connected by some invisible tether, the three whirled. They looked at the approaching pair, then back at Trevor. The air seemed to leak out of them, one at a time. By the time Alton and Grimm rode up in a cloud of dust, they stood like three dejected victims of some great loss.

'What's goin' on here?' the marshal demanded.

The gunman from the Scythe made

one desperate attempt. 'Boy, I'm glad to see you, Marshal,' he said, a little too loudly. 'Killian here's accusin' us o' stealin' H-X calves. Fact is, we're just tryin' to get these ringy ol' cows to let 'em suck. They just went an' got sore, is all. Calves is gonna starve if we don't make the cows let 'em suck. You know that. There ain't nothin' wrong with that.'

Trevor cut in. 'They're H-X calves, Dave. I tracked 'em all the way from our range where they roped 'em. If we take 'em back there, they'll mother up just fine, without havin' to hog-tie the cows to make 'em let 'em suck.'

The marshal looked back and forth from the trio to Trevor, then to the calves, then to the tied cows, still bawling their defiance. Then he said, 'Well, first things first. You boys shuck off them gunbelts an' let 'em drop.'

They all hesitated. The gunman among the trio spoke again. 'What for? You arrestin' us fer somethin'?'

'Not yet. I just like to know nobody's

gonna try somethin' when I ain't lookin'. Now shuck 'em.'

With another moment's hesitation they all complied. The marshal spoke again.

'Now untie them cows and the calves. Let's see if they know who Momma is.'

Two of the trio looked at the third, who had assumed leadership. He shrugged his shoulders. It took only a matter of minutes until all six animals were untied.

The calves ran at once to the cows. The cows sniffed each calf in turn, then turned away from them. One of the calves ran to a cow and tried to nurse anyway. The cow promptly butted the calf away.

'Don't look like sore teats to me,' the marshal observed. 'They ain't even lettin' the calf get close enough to find out whether it hurts. They just don't seem to think them's their calves.'

'Aw, they're just still riled up from a-bein' tied up,' the gunman argued.

'Well, now, that's another point,' the marshal responded. 'Since when do you have to tie the calf up to get the cow to claim it? Seems to me the calf would be plumb anxious to get to the cow.'

The three Scythe hands looked mutely at each other, all at a loss for words. The marshal spoke again. 'You boys best haze them calves over to H-X county. Let's see what they do if they find the cows these fellas think they belong to.'

The three again looked at each other helplessly. The odds had changed dramatically, even without the added weight of the badge one of the men wore. They shrugged, and moved to haze the calves.

It took a long time for the calves to be herded all the way back. The whole way Alton, Trevor and the marshal stayed behind the trio, watching warily. The marshal had collected their gunbelts from the ground and draped them from his own saddle horn, but they were all painfully aware of the possibility of a hideout gun.

When they finally reached H-X range they found the three cows, still plaintively bawling for their calves. The calves they were hazing began to respond to their call even before the cows spotted them, picking up their pace and bleating in reply. When the cows spotted them, then began running to meet the calves.

It took only moments for each cow to identify and claim her calf. The famished calves began nursing feverishly. Within minutes the cows had quieted, and stood contentedly chewing their cuds while their calves filled their bellies.

The marshal spoke. 'Well, boys, looks like you'd best take a ride to town.'

'What for?' the gunman demanded.

'Sure looks to me like a clear-cut case o' calf stealin',' the marshal said. 'You boys is under arrest fer rustlin'.'

'You can't do that!' the gunman insisted. 'We just made a mistake, that's all. Besides, if you try to pull somethin' like that, Pashenka'll take your town apart. There ain't no way you're man enough to keep us locked up.'

'We'll see,' Grimm replied, his face matching his name. 'I been waitin' a long time to get somethin' nice an' clear-cut to call your outfit on. I think we just got it.' He drew his gun and pointed it in the general direction of the three. 'Trevor, you ease up there an' tie these boys' hands behind their backs, then relieve 'em o' them rifles, an' check 'em for any hideout guns.'

Trevor complied silently, making sure each was securely bound. He knotted the reins of each and hooked them over the saddle horn. Then he used his own lariat to make a lead rope for all three mounts. He took the collected rifles to Grimm.

'You carry 'em,' Grimm responded. 'I'd appreciate it if you boys would ride along. I don't look for no trouble, but I'd feel better knowin' you're backin' my play.'

'The real fun'll come when Pashenka finds out we locked up three of his boys,' Alton observed.

'I'm countin' on it,' the marshal said softly. 'I'm countin' on it.'

12

The short cavalcade created as much of a stir as might have been expected. Alton Huxford led the way, holding the lead rope that strung out the three Scythe mounts behind him. Each of those mounts held a disconsolate cowboy, hands bound behind his back. Behind the trio of captives the marshal and Trevor rode side by side.

By the time they made their way to the marshal's office and jail, a crowd had assembled. 'What's goin' on, Marshal?' somebody called from the crowd.

Marshal David Grimm stopped and faced the crowd. He scanned the faces for indications of support or resistance. He said, 'These three boys was caught red-handed stealin' H-X calves, an' puttin' 'em on Scythe cows. I'll be holdin' 'em till the circuit judge comes through, then they'll be tried on charges o' rustlin'.'

A moment of incredulous silence followed, then another voice spoke up from the crowd. 'Pashenka ain't gonna take kindly to that idea.'

The marshal shrugged. 'I 'spect he'll have to answer as well,' he said. 'It seems unlikely these boys was stealin' calves for Pashenka without orders. We'll have some questions to ask him.'

The voice spoke up again. 'He really ain't gonna like that,' with heavy accent on the 'really'.

Grimm smiled tightly. 'I 'spect you're right. And if you're the one gettin' set to go ridin' out there and tell 'im all about it, get goin'. You tell 'im for me that his days of runnin' roughshod over this town an' this county is all done. From now on, he'll answer to the law like everyone else.'

The man who had been doing the talking whirled and almost ran towards the livery barn. By the time the marshal had answered a couple more questions and taken the prisoners inside, the man rode out of the livery barn, heading towards the Scythe Ranch at a gallop.

Trevor watched him ride out, staring after him thoughtfully until he was out of sight. Then he turned and walked to the Mercantile Store. As he walked in the door, Millie ran to him, throwing her arms around him. Taken aback, Trevor instinctively wrapped his own arms around her, but said, 'Whoa, here! What's got you all worked up?'

She loosened her grip enough to tip her head back and stare up into his eyes. 'Oh, Trevor,' she said, 'Alton rode in with his horse almost ridden to death, got the marshal and a fresh horse and rode out again. He said you were tracking three Scythe hands that had stolen some cattle or something. I was so afraid you'd be dead before he could catch up with you again!'

A mischievous gleam flashed in Trevor's eye. 'Well, now, if I'd known it'd get this kind o' response, I'd have had 'im ride in here with some sort o' message a long time ago.'

Millie blushed, suddenly remembering the impropriety of such a public display of affection, especially since Trevor had not really expressed any intentions towards her. He kept his arms around her, however, refusing to allow her to pull away.

'Matter o' fact, I think I'll just stand here thisaway fer an hour or two,' he announced, 'just to see if I like it.'

She moved her arms down and poked him abruptly in the ribs on both sides. He grunted and jumped backward, releasing her. She smiled impishly. 'Well, so much for that promise,' she said.

'You cheated!' he remonstrated. 'You know I'm ticklish.'

She shrugged. 'All's fair in love and war.'

'Yeah? Well, which is this?'

Her eyes went soft and moist as she looked into his suddenly serious gaze. 'I was hoping it was love,' she said softly.

He started to reply, but a catch in his

throat prevented his saying something. He reached for her, and her move to respond was cut short by her mother's words. 'If you two lovebirds can hold off on all the mush for a while, there's likely a war to think about too.'

Trevor swallowed his intense dis-appointment. He ached with an irresistible desire to hold Millie, hug her to himself and never let go. He could see the same desire in her eyes, but her mother's voice was insistent. 'Pashenka will be ridin' into town with every hand he's got to get them boys of his out of jail. He can't afford to let the town think we can stand up to him. If they go to trial, he's all done around here, and he knows it.'

Trevor tore his eyes away from Millie with great difficulty. 'Whatd'ya mean?'

Matilda's eyes wore a triumphant expression. 'He ain't got title to an acre of that ranch,' she asserted.

'He ain't?'

She shook her head emphatically. 'Not an acre. He just took it all from its rightful owners, run them out of the county or killed them, and just took it over, daring anyone to stand up against him.'

Trevor frowned. 'You mean that whole ranch isn't even legally his?'

'That's exactly what I mean.'

'Then why hasn't anyone called him on it?'

'Who?' she asked bluntly. 'Anyone that tried ended up dead. After a while everyone knew you can't stand up to Pashenka and survive. That is, until you came along. The threat against him now isn't that three of his hands are going to be tried for rustling. He don't care two cents for them. He'll just hire more to take their place, and it doesn't matter to him if they hang. The threat is that you've convinced people they dare to stand up to him. If he lets that stand, he's finished and he knows it.'

Trevor pondered the information. It was difficult to concentrate on it with Millie standing so close beside him. He could smell the soft fragrance of her hair. He kept stealing glances at the smooth perfection of her face, the line of her jaw, the lift of her chin. She turned and looked up at him. He almost lost himself again in the deep pools of her eyes. He forced himself back to the subject.

'So whatd'ya think he'll do?' he asked Matilda.

Impatience flashed in Matilda's eyes. 'I already told you, if you were listening to me instead of making moon eyes at my daughter. He'll ride into town with every hand he has, take his men out of the jail, and kill anyone that gets in his way.'

'He can try,' Trevor responded.

'He will try,' Matilda assured him. 'I think it's time to make the stand we've been talking about. It's even better than trying to respond when he attacks one of the homesteads. We know where he will come, so we can have everyone come into town, and be ready for him.'

It dawned suddenly on Trevor what she was proposing. 'You mean get all the homesteaders an' such into town, an' wait fer 'em to show up?'

'Exactly!' Matilda exulted. 'It's made-to-order. He can't prevail against the combined force of all the homesteaders and ranchers that were at the meeting.'

Trevor turned the idea over and over in his mind. He decided she was right. It was tailor-made for their purposes. 'Can you get word out to all of 'em?' he asked.

She nodded. 'I already sent Wad Bursell out with the word,' she said. 'The nearest of the homesteaders should start arriving in town in less than three hours. When enough of them are here, it will be up to you to deploy them.'

'To what?'

'Deploy them. Put them where they can defend the jail, watch for Pashenka's approach, and fight a battle if need be, without shooting into each other.'

Trevor digested the new ideas. 'I ain't never done nothin' like that there,' he protested. 'I can fight with the best of 'em, but I ain't no general or nothin'. I can't tell no one else how and where to fight.'

'You must,' Matilda insisted. 'You are the one they all look up to, because you have stood up to Pashenka and his bullies. They will take orders from you.'

'I ain't got no idea where to start somethin' like that,' he protested again.

She sighed heavily. 'Here, let me make a suggestion. What would happen if you put two men over there . . . '

She laid out a plan she had obviously already worked out in her mind. Trevor listened with amazement as the pieces were put into place for a solid plan to defend the town against however many men Pashenka brought with him. He could see no flaw in it.

Millie finally laid a hand on his arm. 'If you'd walk me home, I'll get supper. There will be plenty of time to start putting men where you want them after supper.' Her tone turned gently sarcastic. 'They will meet at the saloon, I'm sure.'

Matilda nodded her agreement and turned back to her duties in the store. Trevor walked out with Millie, trying hard to keep his mind on the coming conflict.

By two hours after supper enough men had assembled to begin the town's defences. The marshal offered to deputize each man, making their actions legal and official. He suggested they set the men up in shifts, however, so some were always sleeping while others kept watch. He also ordered the bartender to put a two-drink limit on every man. That way they would have fresh, sober men available.

More men drifted into town as the night wore on. Shortly after dawn, still others arrived. There was no sign of Pashenka or his men. Trevor spent the day with Millie, hoping the inevitable battle would never come. He was amazed at the number of things they thought of to talk about. She even began showing him how to make letters of the alphabet, promising it would be easy for him to learn to read. 'I'da learnt it a long time ago, if'n I'd had the chance,' he assured her.

'Well, I'm glad you didn't,' she offered.

'You are? How come?'

'Because if you had learned it earlier, I wouldn't get to teach you.'

The day faded into darkness with no sign of the Scythe Ranch or its hands. The second night passed equally uneventful. By dawn of the next day, Trevor was clearly worried. The marshal was as confused by the lack of response as he. Trevor walked to the Mercantile Store to share his concerns with Matilda.

As he approached the store, he spotted a rider nearing town, riding hard. He watched until he recognized him as one of the hands from the Scythe Ranch. He stepped into the middle of the street and waited. The rider slid his horse to a stop right in front of him. 'You're Killian?'

'I am.'

'I just rode into town to tell you, then

I'm lightin' out. I ain't got no part o' what they're doin'.'

'Who's doin' what?'

'Pashenka, he's hoppin' mad. Worst I ever seen 'im. He knows you're waitin' for him here, so he can't come after the boys. So he's just now headin' out with the whole outfit to go after Huxford. He says that'll get at you better'n anythin'. I ain't got no truck with fightin' women an' kids, so I lit out. Thought you oughta know.'

With that he turned his horse and galloped away. Trevor raced to the crowded livery barn and hurriedly saddled his horse. He took no time to fill his canteen or take supplies. He simply yielded to the urgency to get to the H-X, to rescue Lavina and the children from the attack that must surely be taking place. He jammed his spurs into his horse's sides, offering an unaccustomed prayer that he would not be too late.

In his heart, he was almost certain he already was.

13

He never saw it coming.

Trevor rode low over his horse's neck. The wind in his face blew his hat brim up flat against the crown. The horse's long legs reached out, eating up the ground. Trevor's eyes were fixed on the horizon, where the road disappeared over the next ridge.

With every stride of the horse his anxiety increased. He should have suspected Pashenka would not make an all-out assault on the town. He knew he himself was the Scythe Ranch's prime target. He was the one who had organized the resistance. He was the one who had defied Pashenka and survived — so far. They would not come against him while he was in town, surrounded by the aroused owners of half the homesteads and small ranches in the area.

He tried to force unwanted images from his mind. In spite of his best efforts, he continually saw flashes of a burning ranch house, of Alton cut down in the yard, of Leah facing again her worst fears.

He heard in his mind Leah's fervent thanks for the talk he had with her parents. Lavina had gone to Leah and poured out her soul in apology for her viciousness, and asked for a chance to atone for it. Leah was thrilled, and told him it was like belonging, finally, to the family she had always wanted. Now, he saw images in his mind of the whole family lying where they had tried in vain to defend their home.

He resisted the urge to spur his horse. If he made him run faster, he could not possibly last the entire distance to the ranch. The sick feeling in his stomach assured Trevor that any speed would be too slow. He had stayed in town too long. He had underestimated Pashenka.

His mind was entirely too focused on

where he was going. He thought of nothing but his fear. Long experience should have told him never to succumb to tunnel vision. His panic at believing he had been outwitted, that the Huxford family were in jeopardy, made him careless.

He was five miles from town. The road led into a defile that meandered its way through jumbled boulders, along a steep cliff, to a high mesa. From there it followed a hogback down into the next, higher valley. The Big Horn Mountains loomed as a back-drop behind the road's steady climb in altitude.

As he approached the defile, he suddenly caught the glint of sunlight on metal, high up to his right. He jerked his head up to look more closely. Just as he did, he heard his horse grunt. The animal's gait changed perceptibly.

A flat sound, like the crack of a tree limb breaking, carried on the breeze from behind and to his left. Instinctively he knew the sound of a rifle. He spun his head. A wisp of smoke dissipated from a clump of brush two hundred yards away.

A slight tug wiggled the hat on his head. He snapped back around just in time to see a similar wisp of smoke from the top of a boulder, above and to the right of the road. His horse's gait faltered, then picked up again, laboured now.

Trevor swore. He jerked his carbine from the saddle scabbard. The horse stumbled, then tried to resume running. He stumbled again as Trevor jacked a cartridge into the chamber. The air around Trevor's head seemed filled with the buzz of angry bees passing over and around him. He dived from the horse, hit the ground and rolled. The horse collapsed almost as he left the saddle.

Trevor scrambled into a niche behind a large boulder. His horse lay in the road. His eyes were open. His tongue lolled out of his open mouth. Blood soiled the ground in three places at the edge of his body. Trevor swore again.

Bullets gouged pieces off of the boulder he crouched behind. Some ricocheted with mournful whines into the distance. Others thwacked flatly into softer spots on the rock. He was two hundred feet from the base of the cliff. Straight behind his position the cliff had a narrow defile that opened back into it a few feet. Large boulders lay strewn about as if a giant castle had collapsed.

He tried to peer around the boulder he cowered behind. As his head rose above its cover, half a dozen bullets chipped pieces of rock within inches of his face. He was showered with painful bits of stone shattered from its surface.

He wiped a hand across his face, noticing distractedly the blood on his hand. He looked back towards the relative shelter of the cliff. Making an abrupt decision, he wheeled away from his cover. Running and dodging, crouched as low as he could manage, he darted from rock to rock. The hidden rifles picked up to a feverish pace. Dirt and bits of rock kicked up all around him. His hat flew from his head. Instinctively he grabbed it as he ran. Something tugged at his shirt below his arm.

He made one last desperate dive behind a pair of matched monoliths that guarded the entrance to the shallow niche in the face of the cliff. He landed in soft dirt. A small cloud of dust erupted from his landing. The rifle fire abated.

He sat up and surveyed his situation. He looked straight up. The cliff at this point leaned outward, making it impossible for anyone to climb above and shoot down into his shelter. Steep rock walls on either side afforded protection from his flanks. The only approach to his position was from the front, where the jumble of rocks and the two gigantic monoliths of stone provided a shield from his enemies' fire. It was as good a place for a stand as he could have hoped for.

He glanced at the sky. There were

probably four hours of daylight left. He could hold them off until dark. Then it would be a matter of their needing only to approach quietly enough to be too close for him to fight off their number.

He assessed the strength of his opponents. He put his hat on his rifle and moved it into view at the side of the rock tower he sat behind. Immediately it was met with the fire of five or six rifles that he could distinguish. One of them succeeded in adding a third hole to the crown. 'Good shots,' he admired drily. 'Quick, too.'

He appraised his supplies. For the rifle he had only the twelve cartridges in the magazine of the Winchester 1873. For his Colt he had its six rounds, plus roughly twenty in his cartridge belt. 'Not much fer a stand-off,' he muttered.

He worked his way to a spot where he could peer through the narrow crack between the two stone towers that stood like twin sentinels guarding his position. He watched the narrow area of boulders beside the road within his field of vision. It was not more than two minutes until he spotted movement. Part of a face showed for an instant, then moved back into cover.

He raised his rifle and rested it against the stone. He watched over the top of the barrel for the face to reappear. In just a few minutes it did so, as one of the Scythe riders raised up to aim his own rifle at Trevor's hiding place. As he came into view, Trevor squeezed the trigger.

The man was rising into view as he fired. At the recoil of the rifle, the man stood suddenly to full height. He threw his arms up and outwards. His head flew back. He went with it, falling backwards out of sight. Trevor nodded with satisfaction. He ducked back into his cover as a new fusillade erupted. He sat behind the rock, smiling tightly. 'That's one,' he said.

He moved to the left edge of his small circle of protected space. Finding a niche that showed as little of his own face as possible, he again watched for movement. The first movement he saw was much farther away than his attackers. A lone horseman had emerged on the road leading from town. The horseman stopped. A nearer movement caught Trevor's eye. The tip of a hat showed in a nest of boulders on the far side of the road, up the boulder-strewn slope. He guessed it would be the one who put the first shot into his horse. He lined his rifle up on the spot and again waited. He saw the hat's tip again. As he watched, part of a man's face appeared at the side of a huge rock. He squeezed his trigger. The face disappeared instantly. Whether he hit him or not he had no way to know.

Again, there was an instant response from nearly a dozen rifles. Bullets whined away into the air and splatted wickedly against rock around him. He moved cautiously back to a spot where he could see the road. The lone horseman was gone. Disappointment knifed through him. 'Thought maybe it'd be somebody that'd lend a hand,' he muttered.

It was hot. Dust hung in the air, kicked up by the sporadic hail of bullets probing his niche. He licked his lips. They tasted dusty. 'Well, at least I got some shade.'

He sat down with his back against the rocky cliff. He looked around and picked up a small pebble. He wiped it as clean as he could on his pants leg, and put it in his mouth, knowing it would make his mouth water slightly, alleviating the sense of thirst. Every few minutes he moved to a different spot and looked for a target. Every time he fired he drew a withering fire in response, but no bullets could penetrate his cover. Every time he fired he also drew one shell closer to being out of ammunition. He knew his pistol was almost worthless at the range he was firing. He assumed his attackers were also counting his rifle shots. Few people carried extra cartridges in their pockets. When he left his horse they could safely assume he had only the rifle shells his magazine could hold.

'They'll move in as soon's they figger I'm outa shells,' he told himself.

The shadows grew longer. He knew he'd hit at least two men. He thought he may have hit one or two others. As best he could remember, he was down to two shots for the rifle. There was no way to slip away unseen.

He sighed heavily. 'Well, I guess my best chance is to wait fer dark, just like they're a-doin'. Then maybe I can crawl off over there around them rocks an' slip out. I 'spect my chances are somewheres between slim an' none,' he said aloud, 'an' I wouldn't be s'prised if Slim's already gone south.'

The shadow of the cliff stretched clear across the road. Only the tip of the ridge on the far side still shone with sunshine. The shadows around the rocks grew thicker. 'Dark in less'n half an hour,' he said.

Another sound intruded. Men began

to yell something he could not understand. Rifle fire erupted again, but no bullets whined and ricocheted around him. He risked peering around his protecting monoliths of stone. No fusillade met his appearance. The attention of his attackers seemed to have been diverted.

He stood cautiously to peer past the boulders. A large group of horsemen had arrived and fanned out in a large half-circle, approaching his attackers from the rear. The tables had abruptly been turned. Attackers were now the ones being attacked. They were all scrambling feverishly out of the rocks and towards their horses.

Gunfire kept up a staccato clatter as the two groups snapped off hurried shots at one another. One of the Scythe crew went down, then a second. Then one of the new group yelled and fell to the ground, screaming in fear and pain.

Trevor spotted Pashenka. He was easy to identify by his size and shape, racing for the black Morgan gelding he favoured. Trevor jerked his rifle to his shoulder and snapped off a shot, with little hope of connecting. The rancher was six hundred yards away and running. All Trevor could do was lob a bullet high enough to try for a lucky fluke. It was not to be. The rancher leaped with surprising agility into the saddle and spurred his horse to a run.

He was followed in a cloud of dust by the survivors of his crew. Trevor counted four empty saddles as they raced away.

He walked cautiously out of his cover. From the attacking group a single rider broke away and rode at a gallop towards, him. He recognized Millie at once. She slid to a stop beside him as he reached the road. She leaped from the saddle into his arms.

'Oh, Trevor!' she gasped, her arms around him, squeezing as if to enfold him completely into herself. 'I was so afraid we wouldn't get here in time.'

He returned the hug for a moment, then drew back. 'Was that there you what come up the road an' left again?'

She nodded mutely. Tears flooded her eyes, spilling down her cheeks. 'I didn't even have a gun! I was so afraid when you rode out of town without saying anything, and I started after you. Then I heard all the shooting, so I stopped and looked. I saw your horse in the road. I couldn't tell it was your horse; but I knew it must be. I decided Pashenka tricked you into leaving town, so he could get you alone and kill you. But I knew you weren't dead. They were still shooting, and you were shooting back from the rocks over there, and I rode back to town and told everyone what was happening, and all the men grabbed their horses and came running out here, and I was so afraid we would be too late and I just knew you were going to already be dead before we got here and oh, Trevor I couldn't stand it if anything happened to you and . . . '

Trevor was overwhelmed with the sudden need to stop the torrent of her words. He considered putting a hand over her mouth. Then he decided his own lips would do a better job. It worked splendidly. There was no objection from Millie.

14

'It's the only thing that'll keep it from a-bein' an all-out war.'

Marshal Grimm scowled at Trevor. 'It's suicide, that's what it is. You'll just get yourself killed, then we'll have to go ahead and do what I have to do anyway.'

Trevor shook his head again. 'I 'spect I can do it.'

'You're crazy as a bedbug,' the marshal disagreed. 'They gotta know we'll come after 'em. Pashenka finally stepped over the line. The law has a clear shot at 'im now. They know the little guys are organized, and that they're all in town. They already put his outfit on the run. They'll be forted up at the ranch, just waitin', knowin' the whole bunch is on the way.'

'That's my whole point,' Trevor agreed. 'But they're expectin' an all-out attack, just like we was expectin' in town. They'll be watchin' for a big bunch o' folks, comin' hell-bent fer leather. Instead o' that, I'll slip in alone, stick a sock in Pashenka's mouth to keep 'im quiet, an' haul 'im outa there. Once he's in town, locked up in your jail, we kin just tell the rest o' his outfit to light outa the county or git locked up too. They'll leave. It ain't like they's got a lot o' loyalty to the brand or nothin' there. Most of 'em's just boys what hired on fer big money durin' the fight, an' figger to move on anyhow.'

The marshal digested this uncommonly long speech from the drifter. Finally he said, 'What's your stake in this? You just hired on with Huxford two or three months ago. Why are you willing to risk your own life to go get Pashenka and bring him in?'

Trevor frowned thoughtfully. 'Well, it's got sorta personal. It's got some to do with Millie. Pashenka went an' killed 'er pa.'

'For rustling,' the marshal finished.

Trevor shook his head. 'He wasn't no rustler. That there was just like what they did with Huxford, brandin' one o' their own calves with the other fella's brand, then accusin' him o' doin' it. Only with Huxford I was there to stop 'em. Ralston wasn't so lucky. He was all alone, so they just hanged 'im. Sorta hard fer 'im to tell you what really happened after he's left danglin' from a tree limb.'

The marshal nodded thoughtfully. 'I pretty much knew that was the way it was done,' he agreed, 'but there was nothing I could do.'

'You coulda leaned on 'em some,' Trevor argued.

The marshal sighed. 'Maybe.'

Trevor pressed it. 'You coulda leaned on 'em enough to at least make folks start askin' questions. Like how come he don't even have title to the land his buildin's is on.'

The marshal's head raised. 'He doesn't have title?'

'Not the way I heard it.'

'Who holds the deed to that land?'

Trevor shrugged. 'Didn't think to ask. Just heard it wasn't Pashenka.'

The marshal stared into nothing as he pondered the information. Then he brought himself back to the present with a shrug. 'Well, anyway, I don't think it'll work, tryin' to bring in Pashenka all by himself. But, if you're bound to try it, I'll deputize you, and I'll go with you.'

Trevor shook his head. 'One might get in an' out. Two's only half as like to make it.'

Grimm shook his head. 'One ain't enough to cover your back. Or to knock Pashenka in the head if we need to, and still keep it quiet. No, we'll do it together or not at all.'

In the end the two rode out together. It was mid-afternoon as they rode past the Mercantile Store. Trevor fought down the urge to stop in and tell Millie where he was going. Actually, he wanted to do a little more than that. He thought one more taste of her lips would go a long way towards making the trip out and back with Pashenka more enjoyable.

He had never been in love before. As a matter of fact, he reflected, he had never really had any dealings with any woman before, except the casual relationship between him and a rancher's wife and family, or the occasional wife of another cowboy. Married cowboys were rare, and most of the women he had known were the inevitable ones that populated the saloons and Hog Ranches.

He had only visited one of the Hog Ranches once. The nature of the place made it readily obvious only those truly desperate for a drink or a woman would be found there. He certainly wasn't in strong enough need of either one to be remotely interested in what he found offered.

When he met Millie his whole world had changed. He was drawn to her as if by some great, irresistible magnet. It had seemed incredible to him that she shared his sense of attraction. The relationship between them grew so easily and naturally he decided some unseen hand had destined them for each other, and they simply belonged together. He was at a loss for any other explanation.

Instead of yielding to his impulse to stop in, he rode on past, carefully looking straight ahead. That was why he failed to see both Millie and her mother standing inside the window, watching their passing.

It was dusk as they reined in on the hill overlooking the Scythe Ranch headquarters. Even in the dimming light, it was a magnificent view. The mountains to the north and west gave a perspective of snow-capped grandeur to the whole valley. The cottonwood trees and brush marked out the course of the creek that spilled out of those mountains and crossed the broad valley. Beaver dams on the creek made areas of marshy ground that stretched sometimes half a mile wide. Here and there clumps of quaking aspen trees, groves of cedar, and farther away, areas timbered with pine and spruce gave variant patches of green to the vista's nearer shades of sagebrush and grasses.

Nearer to them, on a rise overlooking the creek, but sheltered by a higher hill to the southwest, the buildings sat. The house was on the eastern edge of the rise, facing east. It was made solidly of logs, set on a rock foundation. A broad porch fronted the house, with its roof coming down low enough to afford protection from all but the most wind-driven snows. The windows were real glass.

Behind the house were four other buildings. It was easy to identify the horse barn, the bunkhouse and the cookhouse. As the pair sat their horses in the shelter of a thicket of plum bushes, Trevor asked, 'What's that fourth buildin'?'

'Looks like an outhouse.'

'Not that one!' Trevor exclaimed. 'I do know an outhouse when I see one.

Even a three-holer like that there must be. Why would they make a three-holer?'

'Save time a-waitin', I s'pose,' the marshal conjectured.

Trevor snorted. 'I'd rather wait than sit in a line o' fellers, seein' who can stink the worst.'

The marshal grinned. 'I don't s'pose it'd make a whole lot of difference. In the winter time it wouldn't matter much, 'cause the stink ain't too bad. In the summer the stink's so bad already a little extra ain't gonna be noticed much.'

Trevor grinned in return, warming to the conversation. 'I 'spect you're right. I still don't cotton to linin' up in a row to take care o' that. I'm sorta private-like.'

The marshal almost ignored the response. 'I've heard tell there's folks that pour lime in theirs.'

'What?'

'Lime. It's some sorta powder. Kinda like alkali. You can buy it in hundred pound bags.'

'What's it fer?'

'The stink.'

'What?'

'The stink. They pour some lime down in the hole every week or so. It does somethin' to keep it from stinkin'.'

'You serious?'

'Yup. That's what I've heard.'

'You mean if you use that stuff, that lime, the outhouse won't stink no more in summer than it does in winter?'

'That's what I've heard.'

Trevor pondered it for a long moment in silence. 'Whatd'ya know!' he marvelled. 'What'll they think of next!'

'Puttin' 'em inside,' the marshal responded.

'What?'

'You sure say 'What?' a lot.'

'What'd you say 'bout puttin' the outhouse inside?'

'They do back east, I've heard.'

'You're puttin' me on! How could they stand it?'

218

'Don't stink none, they say. Some-body figured out a new idea to hook up pipes to everyone's house. Just in cities, mind you. Then they put the outhouse inside, an' after you use it everything goes in the pipe. Then they pour in water or somethin' to wash it on down the pipe.'

Trevor pondered it for a long moment. 'Don't the stink just come back up the pipe?'

The marshal shrugged. 'I'd s'pose it would. Maybe they put a lid on it.'

'Maybe,' Trevor agreed. 'I think I'd rather step outside than lift that lid, though. An' right inside the house! Aw, I ain't sure I believe that there at all. You're just tryin' to put one over on me.'

The marshal shrugged again. 'It's what I've heard. How you figgerin' to do this?'

'I been thinkin' while you been jawin' 'bout bringin' the outhouse inside. See that main gate comin' into the yard?'

'They'll likely have a guard posted there, listenin' fer anyone a-slippin' up in the dark.'

'Most likely.'

'Then they'll likely have one on the far side. You still didn't say what that other buildin' is. The one that ain't the outhouse, an' it ain't the barn, an' it ain't the bunkhouse, an' it ain't the cookhouse.'

The marshal chuckled. 'I wondered if you were ever going to get back to that. I don't know.'

'Must be storage o' some sort.'

'We'll slip in right over there.'

'From the crick?'

'Uh huh. Chances are they'll have someone walkin' around the buildin's. We'll have a moon if we wait three or four hours, though. We can watch fer 'im an' rap 'im on the head or somethin', then we'd oughta be able to make the house without wakin' anyone up.'

'Pashenka ain't the only one in the house.'

'He ain't? Who else lives in the house?'

'Kelby. He's the foreman, an' Pashenka's righthand man. Sometimes they got women, too. Bring 'em all the way from Casper, I hear. Keep 'em here a week or two, just for Pashenka an' Kelby, not for the hands, then send 'em off again.'

'You 'spect there's any there now?'

'I doubt it. Ain't seein' no sign of it, anyway,' the marshal replied. 'And with all the things they're involved in right now, it's not likely. No, I think it'll just be Kelby and Pashenka.'

Trevor pondered the information. 'You plan to arrest both of 'em?'

'Yup.'

'That'll make two to get out without wakin' up the crew.'

'Yup.'

The sinking feeling in Trevor's stomach assured him that would be more than just twice as difficult.

Time passed slowly. The marshal obviously needed a smoke, but dared not risk it. The dusk thickened into the blackness of night. A light flared by the gate to the yard, as the guard lit a cigarette. The match was extinguished, leaving the soft glow of the cigarette's tip clearly visible. 'Smart fella,' Trevor commented, his voice dripping with sarcasm.

'Suits me fine,' the marshal responded. 'Now if there's a sentry in the yard, it'd be helpful if he'd be dumb enough to do the same.'

As if on cue a match flared in the area between the house and the creek, then reduced to the glow of a second cigarette. 'You got some powerful wishes,' Trevor chuckled.

The marshal stood. 'Couple more hours to wait,' he said, walking some of the stiffness out of his knees. 'Then by the time we're down there an' across the crick, the moon'll be comin' up.'

'Let's go straight in, go faster, an' start now,' Trevor countered.

'What? I thought you wanted to go around by the crick.'

'They got their guards out already. We know where they are, thanks to 'em likin' their smokes so good. We'll have more advantage if we don't wait fer the moon. After it's up, they'll be able to see us.'

Grimm pondered it. He looked in the direction of the now invisible ranch house. 'Let's do it,' he said.

They moved down off the hill slowly, leading their horses. By the main road into the ranch, which they guessed was about two hundred yards from the gate, they tied the horses to a large clump of sage. Then they moved forward slowly and carefully.

A light flared again from twenty yards in front of them, as the guard at the gate lit another cigarette. Trevor acted swiftly. Knowing the man would be temporarily blind to movement in the night by the bright flare of the match, he ran swiftly and silently, straight at him.

The man sensed his approach. He tossed aside his cigarette as he said,

'What — ' The word was cut off by Trevor's gun barrel connecting with his head, just above the ear. He dropped to the ground in a silent heap.

The marshal whispered, 'Tie 'im up and stuff his neckerchief in his mouth. We don't want 'im comin' to an' yellin'.'

Trevor stared at the marshal he couldn't see. 'I ain't got nothin' to tie him with,' he whispered in return.

He felt something touch his hand. He grabbed it, then realized it was a short section of light rope. 'You think o' everythin'?' he whispered.

'Try to,' the marshal confirmed.

He tied the guard swiftly and tightly, thinking ruefully how much his hands and arms were going to hurt if he was left for any length of time. Then he stood and silently approached the yard.

The second guard again obliged them by pinpointing his location. He just couldn't pace the yard without another smoke. They repeated the procedure, eliminating him from their concern.

They stepped on to the front porch of the house and crossed it swiftly. Trevor went in through the front door without hesitating. His pistol was in his hand. Soft light spilled out from the kitchen. He stepped into the doorway and moved to the side as the marshal stepped in beside him.

Pashenka and Kelby were sitting at the table, each holding a cup of coffee. Dirty dishes crowded the tabletop.

'Put your hands where we can see 'em,' Trevor barked.

'You are both under arrest,' Grimm added.

Both men stood slowly, then Kelby's hand streaked for his gun. Trevor was stunned by the man's speed. His gun was already clear of the holster and raising in line with his own body before Trevor could fire. Both guns roared. Gunsmoke billowed in the soft lamplight. The two stared silently at each other for a full heartbeat. Then Kelby's gun slipped from his fingers and clattered to the floor. Kelby followed it to the floor an instant later.

Pashenka's face blanched. Grimm blew out the lamp, plunging the room into darkness. Shouts rose from outside. Trevor jammed his gun barrel against the side of Pashenka's neck. 'Get your hands behind your back or I'll blow yer head off!' he whispered hoarsely.

Pashenka complied, but Trevor could feel the fierce tide of the rancher's anger. Grimm swiftly tied his hands there, then pushed the rancher towards the door. As they started to step out, someone called, 'Hey! Here's Buck! They got 'im hog-tied!'

Another voice called, 'Where's Charley?'

The first voice yelled, 'Check the house.'

Trevor and Dave Grimm stared at each other, straining to see in the near pitch darkness. Trevor came to an abrupt decision. He slugged Pashenka above the ear with his gun barrel. The rancher grunted and sagged forward. He took a step to keep his balance, but did not fall.

Trevor hit him with the gun barrel again. This time the rancher crashed to the floor, upsetting a chair and sending it crashing into the table. Dishes clattered to the floor with a din that could have been heard half a mile away.

'Back door,' Grimm whispered hoarsely.

Both men moved to the door that opened from the kitchen directly into the yard. It was only slightly lighter in the yard, still far too dark to see anything more than three feet away. Voices called from all over the yard.

'C'mon,' Grimm whispered.

He stood away from the house and started walking across the yard. Trevor followed, then jumped as the marshal called out, 'They're in the house! I just heard somethin' crash in there!'

They both stopped and stood. As men began to materialize out of the darkness, the marshal spoke again. 'Who's that over there?'

The attention of the crew, fumbling around in the dark yard, was directed to the house. Grimm started walking backward, away from those who had arrived. Trevor followed closely enough to keep him in sight, even in the dark.

As soon as they were out of vision again, the marshal turned and walked quickly in the direction of the building they had not been able to identify. Trevor figured out what he had in mind. 'Just's well try it,' he whispered.

The wall of the building hulked suddenly in front of them. They stopped quickly, just before they ran into the side of it. Putting one hand on the wall, Trevor followed along to reach the side with the door. There was nobody there that he could sense. Moving as quietly as possible he walked to the single step. He stepped up and tried the door latch. It opened easily. With the marshal right behind him, he stepped into the deeper blackness of the interior and shut the door.

They both listened intently. There was no indication they had been seen. Trevor heaved a deep sigh and holstered his gun. He began moving around the building's single room, trying to determine what it held.

His foot bumped against something hard. He knelt down and felt it. It was a wooden box, about two feet long, a foot wide and a foot high. He felt for the lid and lifted it carefully. Reaching inside he felt rows of hard, round tubular objects, almost a foot long, less than two inches in diameter. He lifted one and hefted it thoughtfully. Then he felt his stomach lurch. He laid it back down carefully and felt around. At once he felt three more of the wooden cases.

'Grimm!' he whispered.

'Yeah?'

'I found out what's in here.'

'What?'

'Dynamite. They got this thing filled with dynamite!'

'What? Dynamite?' Grimm answered,

forgetting to whisper.

'Shhh!'

The marshal returned to his whisper. 'We picked this building to hide out in, an' it's filled with dynamite? One bullet into here and we'll be blowed to kingdom come!'

The sinking feeling in Trevor's stomach assured him that was the one thing most likely to happen, just as soon as the Scythe crew figured out where they were.

15

Trevor wiped the sweat from his forehead. He swallowed hard. The sense of imminent destruction rose up all around, threatening to overwhelm him. 'We're gonna get blowed to kingdom come,' he repeated.

'We gotta get out of here,' the marshal agreed.

They moved quickly to the door and opened it. The sounds of a frantic search filled the yard. Lanterns had been lit, and a couple of the hands were carrying them, held high above their head. Each of them was clearly illuminated.

'Set them lanterns down an' get away from 'em,' somebody across the yard yelled. 'You're a perfect target, carryin' 'em.'

The two men indicated hurriedly sat the lanterns on the ground and ran outside the small circle of yellow light they afforded. Grimm chuckled softly. 'Dumb,' he said. 'Let's get outa here.'

'Wait a minute,' Trevor said.

He picked up one of the cases of dynamite. He placed it just inside the door. Then he took half a dozen sticks of dynamite and piled them against the box, on the side next to the doorway. 'What're you doin'?' Grimm asked.

'Fixin' somethin',' Trevor said.

Trevor turned to the window and stooped over beneath it. He had noticed the window was broken, and pieces of glass lay on the floor. He took a piece of the glass and leaned it against the small pile of dynamite. Then he whispered, 'OK. Let's go.'

Dave Grimm swallowed his questions and followed, moving as silently as he could. The two moved furtively through the darkness, back to the side of the house. Inching slowly along the even greater darkness of its side, they reached the corner. Trevor looked cautiously around it. He could neither see nor hear anything.

He looked towards the east. The sky was lightening perceptibly. 'Almost moonrise,' he whispered, pointing.

'We gotta move now,' Grimm responded.

'Not yet,' Trevor answered. 'I got an idea, but we gotta wait for the first moonlight.'

Still confused, but unwilling to risk any more talk, the marshal shrugged. Trevor moved around the corner of the house and crouched against its wall. Grimm followed. Trevor silently drew his gun and waited.

It was almost fifteen tense minutes of listening to the sounds of the ongoing search before the moon finally became visible. Then it began to rise as a great orange ball above the eastern horizon. As it lifted high enough to begin illuminating the earth, one of the first things its rays fell on was the piece of glass Trevor had propped against the small pile of dynamite.

'Get ready to run fer it,' he whispered.

Suddenly realizing what Trevor was planning, the marshal grinned. He pushed away from the wall, prepared for a sprint that would, hopefully, carry them out of the yard.

Trevor aimed carefully. He squeezed the trigger. His gun roared. Fire spat in a long streak from the end of the barrel. The piece of glass shattered. The small pile of dynamite behind it exploded. In an instant filled with events too swift to separate, the case of dynamite followed, then the rest of the dynamite in the shed. To those watching, it was all one sound. One great, ear-splitting explosion slammed against them. The earth vibrated. The storage building disintegrated, sending pieces of wood, glass and assorted debris flying in all directions. It caught fire immediately.

At the instant Trevor fired, both men sprinted for the edge of the yard. The shock of the explosion was so great the marshal ran right past one of the Scythe crew, standing slack jawed. He still had not realized anyone was near him when Trevor's shot cut him down.

The two men sprinted for their horses. The moon's soft glow barely illuminated anything, but their eyes were accustomed to even greater darkness, and they traversed the ground with little difficulty. They passed the border of the yard. They passed the gate. They reached the road leading away from the ranch. They were less than fifty yards from their horses.

'That's far enough!'

They skidded to a stop, struggling to maintain their balance. Alek Pashenka stepped out from behind a tall clump of sagebrush. He had a gun in each hand, levelled at the pair. Even in the moon's glow Trevor could see the dried blood that caked the side of his head.

He swallowed hard. He knew the slightest move would cause the rancher to shoot. He also knew the rancher would kill him, whether he tried anything or not. He tried to catch

Grimm's eye, to send him some kind of silent signal. If they both drew at once, it was unlikely Pashenka could shoot them both before one of them had a chance to put a bullet in him as well.

Then he remembered how hard the big rancher was to bring down with his gun barrel. He had never hit a man that hard without him being knocked instantly unconscious. If he shot the big Russian, he was equally sure he would manage to fire off several shots before he went down. Unless he could shoot him in the head. But that was too risky, especially in the poor light. If he missed with his first shot, he probably wouldn't even get a second shot. Even if his first shot found a fatal mark, they would probably all three die.

'I figured out where you fellows would be headin',' the rancher gloated. 'So while the boys was stumblin' around the yard, I come strollin' out here to see if I could find your horses. Guess what. I did. Then all I had to do was wait. If the boys didn't find you, you'd just come walkin' right to me.'

'You're still under arrest,' the marshal attempted. 'You'd best throw down the gun. It's all over now, no matter what happens. I've already sent a telegram to the governor asking for help. If necessary he will send the army. You can't fight the army.'

Unexpectedly Pashenka laughed. 'You got guts, I'll give you that,' he admired. 'But it won't work. All I got to do is show 'em how you was hooked up with this here rustler. Now I can even show 'em how you came out here and tried to blow up my whole ranch. It won't take much to convince 'em, with you boys dead.'

'It's not your ranch. It's my ranch.'

All three men jumped at the voice from the darkness. Pashenka looked wildly around, trying to find and identify it. 'Who's out there?' he demanded.

Trevor suddenly recognized Matilda's voice. 'The owner of this ranch,' she replied. 'You've been squatting on it long enough.'

'Ralston?' Pashenka asked.

Matilda didn't answer. Instead she said, 'You murdered my husband. You stole my ranch. You destroyed my husband's good name. You have no more right to live.'

As she talked, Pashenka listened closely, trying to pinpoint her position. As he did, the moon's continuing strength illuminated more and more, until he finally picked out her outline in the brush beside the road. The moon's rays glinted on the steel of a double-barrelled shotgun. She held it against her shoulder, watching the rancher over its sights.

Pashenka moved more quickly than Trevor thought a man that size could move. He whirled towards her, firing with both guns. The shotgun against Matilda's shoulder roared. Guns leapt into the hands of both Trevor and the marshal, firing at almost the same time.

The big Russian's body was lifted

from his feet and hurled backward by the double load of buckshot. He jerked as several bullets from the two men's guns slammed into him. He collapsed into a dark heap at the edge of the road.

Trevor saw Matilda wilt. He sprinted to her, holstering his gun as he ran. She dropped the shotgun. She collapsed into his arms as he reached her. He felt something warm and sticky on her back. He pulled his hand away and looked at it. It was covered with blood.

Matilda looked up into his eyes. She opened her mouth. 'My, my ranch,' she croaked.

'Do you mean the Scythe is your place?' Trevor asked. 'You got the deed to the Scythe Ranch? That's the place he killed your husband to take?'

She nodded faintly. 'Millie's ranch now. Take, take care of her, Trevor. She . . . '

She convulsed suddenly. A fountain of blood gushed from her mouth. She tried to take a breath, but it only gurgled. She looked up at him. Her eyes glazed over, then stared hollowly at the moonlight.

'What's goin' on out there?' a voice called from the ranch yard.

Trevor laid Matilda down gently and crouched behind a clump of sage. The marshal did the same. Both men again drew their guns. Grimm spoke up. 'Listen up, you boys! This is Marshal David Grimm. Alek Pashenka is dead. Guy Kelby is dead. This land is the legal property of Matilda and Mildred Ralston. It's all over. You boys can saddle up and ride out of the county, or you can stay here and be arrested and tried for rustling, murder and stealing land. What'll it be?'

Trevor held his breath. It seemed an eternity before one of the hands said, 'Who's gonna pay us what we got comin'?'

The marshal responded instantly. 'What you got comin' is a rope or a jail cell. If you really want it, I'll be happy to oblige. Anything else you got comin' you just gotta do without. Now are you gonna ride out, or shall I bring a posse to clean this outfit out?'

There was another long moment of silence. A different voice said, 'My name's Charley, an' I'll take the offer. I'll ride outa here within the hour.'

'Me too,' another voice responded.

After a moment of silence the first voice called out, 'All right. I guess we all will, an' much obliged for the chance.'

The marshal did not respond. His attention was arrested by the rapid rhythm of hoofbeats coming up the road. The moonlight was strong enough now that Trevor recognized Millie before she got there. He called out to her. 'We're here, Millie.'

She hauled her horse to a stop and leapt from the saddle. She ran to him. 'Oh, Trevor, Mother followed you. She's out here somewhere. She's going to try to get even with Pashenka. I know she is. Trevor, you've got to stop her.'

Trevor swallowed. He reached for

her, taking her by both shoulders. 'Millie,' he said softly, 'she already did. She got her revenge, an' she saved me 'n Dave, a-doin' it.'

Even in the moonlight he could see her wide eyes. 'Is she . . . did she . . . is she all right?'

She searched his eyes frantically for a response. The absence of any words telegraphed what Trevor could not bring himself to put into words. She understood perfectly. 'Oh, Trevor! Oh, dear! Oh, no. Oh, dear God, no.'

She melted into his arms. 'Oh, Trevor! Oh, please hold me. Please don't ever let go!'

It was a promise he was most happy to make. It sure felt good to be wanted. He knew he would never be a castoff cowhand again.